Just An Overnight Guest

Just An

Overnight Guest

by Eleanora E. Tate

The Dial Press · New York

Published by The Dial Press
1 Dag Hammarskjold Plaza
New York, New York 10017

Library of Congress Cataloging in Publication Data
Tate, Eleanora. Just an overnight guest.
Summary: When a disruptive and neglected four-year-old
moves in with her family, nine-year-old Margie Carson
has great difficulty adjusting.
[1. Family problems—Fiction. 2. Cousins—Fiction.
3. Afro-Americans—Fiction] I. Title.
PZ7.T21117Ju [Fic] 80-12970
ISBN 0-8037-4225-8 ISBN 0-8037-4223-1 (lib. bdg.)

To my family,
and to Jerry "Flakes" Burrell

Just An Overnight Guest

1

The sun hadn't even climbed up over the rambling rose hedge in Miz Moten's front yard when I woke up. But I could barely wait to get out of my bed and into the backyard to dig up some fishing worms for Daddy.

See, Daddy was home, and when he first came home after a long trip of moving furniture, I knew he would want to take us fishing. We all liked to fish—Momma, my sister Alberta, and me—but Daddy was a long-distance driver for people who needed their furniture moved, and sometimes was away from home as long as two or three weeks. When he did come, he usually wasn't able to stay for much more than the weekend.

When Daddy got back late last night, I was dead asleep. But when I felt his beard scratching my cheek, I woke right up and hugged him hard. Or I thought I did. I sat up in bed, suddenly afraid. Had I just dreamed that Daddy was back?

I threw off my blanket, ran into the living room, opened the door, and looked out. Our ole red Chevy was parked in the front yard again. I put my ear to Daddy's and Momma's bedroom and heard deep *chuz-z-z* snore noises. That was Daddy, all right. Whew! Grinning, I went back to our bedroom—Alberta's and mine—and put on my tennis shoes, blue jeans, and T-shirt.

After what seemed like a year, a splatter of pale light settled in our room. I jumped up and flew out the back-porch door. Dew sparkled everywhere. I ran around the tomato bushes in the backyard and over to the black-berry patch, bent down, and looked around. With my foot I flipped over a couple of musty boards and watched the sowbugs curl into gray and brown balls. A centipede and a slug crawled away. I could have squashed them, but I didn't feel like hurting anything, not today.

Well, I didn't even see an earthworm hole, let alone a worm. I ran back up the dirt path and over to the side of the house, where Momma's castor bean plants grew, and poked around in the dirt with a stick. Not a worm. I sighed. Where were they? Daddy just had to have fat worms for fishing! Finally I gave up and came back in, but nobody but me and the birds outside was up. I took off my tennis shoes and got in bed with my clothes on, but I didn't figure I'd go back to sleep. Why wouldn't somebody get up?

Alberta's softball glove was lying on the floor by her bed. Usually she oiled her glove, popped a softball in it, and tied it up tight to keep the shape. But last night the Liberty Baptist Ladybugs beat us Nubia Missionary All Stars eleven to nothing. She must have been really disgusted with the game. I knew I was, and I was just a bat girl.

While I waited for Daddy to wake up, I got to thinking about how terrible our team played that game. You'd think we would have got at least one run in. But nobody even got a hit! The only player to even make it to first base was Alberta, and that was after the pitcher hit her with a bad throw. Boy, I wished I was a real member of the team. I bet I could sock that ball way over that fence. . . .

The next thing I knew, Alberta was shaking me awake. By the way, Alberta thinks she's cute, and she is, sort of. She's thin and she has freckles and light skin, like Momma. I'm kind of plump and have dark skin. I look more like Daddy, except of course Daddy has a beard and a mustache and he's six foot five. Daddy is big, big.

"Is Daddy up?" I rubbed my eyes as I scrambled out of bed.

Alberta got to frowning. "What're you doing in bed with your clothes on?" she asked.

"I've been out looking for fishing worms," I told her.

"Well, you gotta get up. Momma wants us to go with her to Miz Silk's and pick out some fabric."

I screwed up my face. "Aren't we gonna go fishing with Daddy?"

Alberta started undoing her braids. Her head looked like black springs were growing out of it. "Who cares? I wanna get some cloth, and so does Momma. She said she'd help me sew a new blouse."

"'Cause you want some ole boy like Billy Ray Morgan to grin at you." Alberta used to be crazy about worm hunting, too, until she turned thirteen last month and fell in love with Billy Ray Morgan.

"Oh, girl, you won't miss Daddy. We'll be back before he can even turn over in the bed. And you *know* he's gonna take us fishing."

But I could tell she would be glad when Daddy was awake, because she missed him as much as I did. Well, almost. I was still kind of disgusted about having to leave the house. Going to Miz Silk's Sewing Circle didn't sound like any kind of fun, not today.

Momma came in bubbling, the way she always did when Daddy was home. "Good morning, good morning, good morning!" Momma is an English teacher at Nutbrush High School. She's small and pretty, and men on the street sometimes whistle or holler, "Hey fox!" at her. She always throws her head up and keeps on stepping, but I like for men to flirt with her because I'm proud of the way she looks. Some mothers I know have big stomachs and don't comb their hair nice and their faces are all sunk in.

"Margie, did I hear you get up earlier?" asked Momma as she tucked her blouse into her slacks.

"I was looking for worms, but I didn't find any. Is Daddy up now?"

Momma smiled. "Not yet. I thought in the meantime we'd go to town and then we can have breakfast when he gets up." She winked at me. "And go fishing. It's early still, honey. Your daddy's not going anywhere."

We got washed up and started out for town. The morning was what Miz Moten called cool with warm edges, which was just right for June. It was just right for hoeing, too. Miz Moten was out there in her garden. I knew it was her because I recognized her straw hat and her hoe bouncing up and down above the hedges. I waved, but she didn't see me.

Ahead of us on the sidewalk lay the Sherwoods' dog Rex, waiting for somebody he could chase or bite. Rex was part collie and I bet part wolf, and he got after everybody but me and Daddy. The Sherwoods claimed he wouldn't bite, but doesn't everybody know that dogs have teeth? I hopped ahead of Momma and Alberta.

"Margie, wait up!" Alberta called. She was afraid of Rex and so was Momma. I felt grown then because I knew they wanted me to protect them. So I waited and they caught up and we walked past Rex like nobody's business.

On Main Street we saw Mr. Cranshaw drive his pickup truck over a curb. I thought he was going to tip over, but he didn't. He just drove right on like he hadn't missed a lick. "Goodness," said Momma, "poor thing is having problems, ain't he?"

I giggled. Momma was always telling us that bad English and gossip were not proper.

Miz Silk's Sewing Circle was by Swensen's Dry Cleaners and Laundry. They were little bitty stores stuck between the Malco Theater on one side and Earl's Drugstore on the other. In front of the drugstore sat the sheriff in his patrol car. He was probably getting ready to go in and have a Dr Pepper. He stayed there all the time.

When we got inside the shop Alberta and I wandered around, careful not to touch anything. Momma had taught us long ago to keep our hands to ourselves in stores.

I was at the button rack looking at button cards when I heard a racket: *thud, boom boom!* Boy, did I jump! A little kid was shoving bolts of cloth to the floor, and cloth was unwinding every which way! Ethel Hardisen! I hated that trashy little kid. Nobody liked her or her ole fat, sloppy mother. Ethel broke stuff, stole candy, threw rocks at people. Once she hit me in the back with a piece of concrete. Some folks said she was half white and other folks said she was half Black. To me she was all bad.

"Little girl!" Miz Silk screamed.

"Ethel!" Momma gasped.

I hurried over to Alberta and Momma, who were standing by the yarn tables. I didn't want anybody to think I had done it. Ethel stood in the aisle. There was a frown on her dirty face and she had white crud around her mouth. She eyeballed everybody. Suddenly, screaming her head off, Ethel galloped down an aisle, snatching up patterns, tearing off the covers, and throwing them up in the air. She ran into a table that had a row of glass statues on it, and glass bounced all over the floor.

"Child!" Miz Silk rushed out from behind the counter.

Miz Mary, Ethel's mother, just stared and scratched at a glob of mud on her ankle. Then she let out a sigh that made her big breasts wobble. "Ethel, don't do that," she said real low.

Momma stretched out her arm like she thought she could stop that kid. Ethel flew past Momma just as Miz Orange, one of Momma's friends, walked in. Know what that kid did? Tromped on Miz Orange's bad foot! Miz Orange let out a whoop, which brought Miz Silk's janitor, Mr. Galligore, running out of the back room.

"Catch her, catch her!" Miz Silk pleaded.

Mr. Galligore grabbed Ethel by the shoulder, but when he did, she kicked him on the ankle. He hollered, but he didn't let go.

Everybody started in then. I had never heard so much shouting except at church, and I guess that was different. "It's just a shame you don't take better care of that child," Miz Orange yelled at Miz Mary.

"My shop is in ruins!" Miz Silk moaned. "And you, Mary Hardisen, you'll pay for this!"

"Girl, you better get yourself over here," Miz Mary roared. When Mr. Galligore pushed Ethel to her, Miz Mary twisted up that kid's arm and dragged her out the door, fussing, "And you better shut up, too."

Mr. Galligore tramped after them. "You hold on just a minute!" he shouted, his face red.

For a minute nobody said a word. Miz Orange leaned against a counter to take the weight off the foot that Ethel had tromped. She cleared her throat and put her eye on Momma. "Now, ain't this something!" she exclaimed. "Ain't this *some* thing!"

"Most horrible child I've ever seen," Miz Silk cried.

Momma kept glancing out the door. Alberta and I looked too. "It's a sad situation," Momma finally said. "Let's go, girls."

"Luvenia," Miz Orange said to Momma, "now did you see that?"

"Well, of course I did," Momma snapped.

"When you were four years old you acted just like Ethel," Alberta whispered to me.

I jutted out my chin. "Did not!"

Miz Silk doubled up her fist and shook it at Momma.

"I'm going to call the sheriff! I want that Mary Hardisen in jail!"

"I'm sure we can remedy this situation, Miz Silk," Momma said. "Let me go and talk to her."

"Momma!" Alberta and I yelled together. Was Momma crazy? Go to Hickory Sticks, the white-trash part of Nutbrush? The whole place was weedy, junky, and run-down. The backwaters of the Mississippi River were on one side, and the railroad tracks and a sewage ditch were on the other. I jiggled my legs and pulled on my braids, which I do when I'm annoyed, but Momma didn't pay me any mind.

"I'll go right now. I'm sure she'll get the money to you as soon as she can," Momma went on.

Miz Silk glared at Momma. "And if she can't?"

Momma didn't answer. As soon as we left the store, Alberta said, "Margie and I'll go on home, okay?"

"No, you're both coming with me," Momma said.

"Why've we got to come?" I cried.

"Because I said so. It'll only take a minute for me to talk to Miz Mary and check on Ethel."

"Let the sheriff do it," Alberta grumbled.

I couldn't see why Momma had to go talk to some trashy woman with a rotten kid who pinched and kicked and cussed and tore up people's stores. My face went to pieces.

Momma smoothed back her Afro, sighed, and looked sad. Then she said sternly, "You ought to see how ugly your faces look. Shame on you, Margie, and you, too, Alberta."

I didn't care how my face looked. I wanted to go home. Didn't matter to Momma. Five minutes later we were following her up the street toward Hickory Sticks. Alberta slapped her feet on the sidewalk, and I did, too. Mad! We hurried past the library. I didn't even have a chance to ask if I could wait in there until she and Alberta came back.

"Momma, you know we don't have any business going down to see that ole stinky kid and her ole—"

"Alberta Carson," said Momma, "please close your mouth."

We walked down a road full of chuckholes and oily, smelly water. The houses looked like they would have fallen down if people weren't still living in them. A couple of mangy-looking dogs barked at us.

"It stinks down here." Alberta put her hand up to her nose. I didn't see but two or three patches of grass anywhere, and not a single flower. I was glad we had hollyhocks and marigolds and begonias and green grass growing in our own yard.

"Look at that skinny girl sticking her head out the door," Alberta whispered to me, "over there."

Then farther down the street an old man in a dirty white T-shirt stood on his porch and watched us pass. He snapped his suspenders. "Dirty niggers," I heard him say.

I got hot, but I didn't know what to do. Momma and Alberta stuck their noses up and stared straight ahead. Red dots stood out on their cheeks. So I stuck my nose up, too.

At last we came to a little patched-up trailer set up on concrete blocks. A clothesline with a dirty sheet on it sloped from the roof of the trailer to another cement block on the ground. One of the trailer windows was broken. Alberta and I stared. Who would ever want to live there?

"Come see the name on this mailbox," Alberta said.

I read the name: Mary Hardisen. I peered up at Momma. "Maybe it's the wrong one? Maybe there's two Miz Marys down here, hunh?"

Momma ran her tongue over her lips and took a deep breath. "Come on, girls. We've come to pay a visit. Let's put on our manners."

Alberta shoved me ahead of her. I took Momma's hand and told myself to get ready to be kicked and bit to death. Momma and I walked into the yard.

"Look, Momma!" I pointed to where a pair of black shoes were sticking out by the trailer. We went around to the side and found Miz Mary sitting on a cement block. She had a can of beer in her hand, and another lay by her feet. She was humming "He Holds My Hand." I recognized the tune because our choir sometimes sings that song in church. But we sure didn't sing it like that.

Miz Mary's stringy brownish-red hair hung around her neck and in her face. Her dress was scrunched up between her legs. I stopped being scared and tried not to giggle. Momma squeezed my hand.

"Hey girl," Miz Mary said, smiling at Momma.

Alberta came up behind us. I let go of Momma's hand and whispered to Alberta, "What's she doing calling Momma 'hey girl' like they're friends?"

Alberta shrugged. "I don't know nothin' about nothin' so don't ask me nothin'."

"So how're ya doin'? Boy, that's good beer." Miz Mary held out the can to Momma. "Have a sip, Luvenia."

Momma jumped back. "No, no thanks," she said. "Mary, we need to talk about Ethel."

"Ain't she a no-count thing?" Miz Mary took another drink.

"Margie, quit staring!" Alberta jabbed me in the ribs with her finger, and that made me laugh out loud.

After Momma gave us a don't-make-me-mad look, she asked Miz Mary where Ethel was. "I don't know, hon." Miz Mary waved her fat arm toward the road. "She's around here somewhere."

Momma opened her mouth, closed it, and opened it again. "You don't just let a four-year-old run wild. You've absolutely got to take care of her."

Miz Mary took a couple more swallows from her beer. "Takes money to raise a kid," she replied. She narrowed her eyes at Momma. "I ain't got no husband to pull in good money like yours do. And you got yourself a nice, fine job, especially for a colored woman." She lit a cigarette and blew smoke out of her nose.

Alberta pointed at the trailer. "Ethel's staring at us from that broken window," she told me.

"Where?" I jerked my head around and saw her sticking out her tongue at me. I stuck out mine.

"—or else she's going to call the sheriff," Momma was saying.

"Well, I just don't know what I can do," Miz Mary replied. "I beat her good every time she acts up."

"Don't beat her!" Momma snatched at the beer can like she wanted to throw it away, but Miz Mary tossed it over her shoulder. "Aren't you even going to look for her?"

"She's in the trailer, Momma," said Alberta.

"Then she darn well better stay in there," Miz Mary threatened. When Momma started for the trailer door, Miz Mary said quickly, "No, don't go in there—I ain't cleaned it up yet. When I went out last night that kid just tore up the place."

Momma looked back at Miz Mary like she had eaten something sour that should have been sweet. "You mean you left her alone? For how long?"

"Oh, Luvenia, ain't nothin' gonna bother her. She's stayed by herself all night plenty times."

"You're going to lose that child if you don't watch out," Momma warned her. "They're already saying you're an unfit mother."

Miz Mary narrowed her eyes again. "Maybe I ought to go visit a certain person, hunh? 'Bout time he helped me with that kid, don't you think?"

The freckles on Momma's nose stood out and the red dots on her cheeks got brighter. "If you think seeing that certain person would help Ethel, by all means, go," she said slowly.

"Course, I don't know what I'd do with *her* if I go." Miz Mary nodded toward the trailer. "Guess I could put her in the Children's Home."

"Would you really do that?" Momma asked. She sighed. "Mary, please let me know what you plan to do about Ethel and the damages to Miz Silk's store. Come on, girls."

When we got a little ways off, I said, "She was drinking a lot of beer, wasn't she, Momma? How come you know her?"

"I just happened to meet her a few years ago."

"Sure wish you hadn't," Alberta put in. "I don't want people knowing that you and her are friends."

"Mind your manners, girls," Momma said.

We started back home. Momma was walking fast and I had to trot to keep up with her, but I didn't mind. I was glad to be back over on my own side of town. I put Miz Mary and Ethel out of my mind. I was going home to Daddy.

2

When we got there, I was the first one inside. Daddy was wide awake and sitting on the couch. He had on his old blue-and-white-striped overalls, the ones he had torn up by wearing so much. "Well, my ladies have come back to me," he said.

We fell on him, Alberta and I, and nestled up under his arms, while Momma kissed him on his bearded cheek. I curled the tip of his beard around my fingers. "What'd you bring us, Daddy?" I asked.

"Ready for breakfast?" Momma said.

Daddy winked at me. "Chile, I'm starving."

"Daddy!" I pulled at his big, hairy arm. "What'd you bring?"

Daddy smiled, showing his teeth real white in the middle of his beard and mustache. He was the only father I knew in Nutbrush who had a beard. He looked like that picture of Samson in my Bible. When he patted his overalls like he'd lost something, a piece of paper stuck up out of a front pocket. Alberta and I fought to grab it.

"Oh, Matt, you've already fixed breakfast!" Momma said from the kitchen doorway. "Alberta, Margie! Let your father be!"

Daddy laughed. "Looks like my girls are trying to fix me. Just wait now, just wait." He handed each of us a package wrapped in tissue paper.

Inside mine was a shiny silver necklace with a tiny star and an M dangling on it. Alberta got a necklace with an A. "Now these are handmade," Daddy said. "Here, Bitty Bit, let me help you before you get all tangled up." His big hands closed over mine and fixed the clasp around my neck. "Handmade by an old silversmith in Dubuque, Iowa. A real old man. I sat there for two hours watching him make just one letter."

"Oh, they're beautiful, Matt," said Momma.

"And that ain't all I brought," said Daddy. He picked up a paper sack from behind the couch. "More shells for your collections, ladies."

When Daddy came back from trips he often brought us some kind of shells. I took a big conch shell and a starfish from the sack, and Alberta took all the smaller ones.

"Thank you, Daddy," we said at the same time. We admired each other's presents, but I thought mine were prettier.

"Girls, your daddy has whipped up pancakes and sugar syrup and scrambled eggs and peaches," Momma announced. "Ready to eat?"

I felt so happy. The best times of all were when Daddy came home. I took his hand and followed Momma into the kitchen. "Let's hurry up and eat!" I jabbed a pancake with my fork. "Let's go fishing!"

Well, we all gobbled up breakfast, and Momma didn't even make Alberta and me wash the dishes. Daddy already had all the fishing poles and equipment ready. "Race you to the car!" Daddy yelled.

Alberta and I flew out that door. I won! Momma and Daddy got in the car, laughing and smiling. On the way to the river we stopped by Griger's Baithouse and Grocery Store and bought a box of worms and some pop and some beer.

Ten minutes later we were sitting on the bank of the Mississippi. A long, rust-colored barge carrying coal drifted past and made the waves smack against the banks. I wrinkled up my nose and smelled the river smells of fish and mud and wet sand.

Suddenly my cane pole bent down. When I jerked it

up, nothing happened. A snag? But then a huge fin broke the surface of the water and disappeared. I gripped my fishing pole tightly, but the tip bent lower and lower.

"Pull him in, Bitty Bit, pull him in!" Daddy yelled.

I couldn't swing the pole up over my head and land him. "Daddy! Come help!"

Daddy slipped in the muddy grass trying to get to me. "You musta hooked hold of the river!"

"He's gonna get away, Daddy!"

Momma and Alberta jumped up and ran over to us while Daddy grabbed my line and helped me steer the fish to the shore. My arms ached, but I still held on to my pole.

"Shooo, who said my girl couldn't fish?" Daddy hollered as he lifted the flopping fish out of the water. He threw me a big grin. "This bass must come close to six pounds!"

A six-pound bass! It looked like a whale. Everybody was so proud of me. We fished the rest of the day, and Daddy caught two catfish, but they weren't as big as my bass. Finally we got back in the car and came home. I beat Alberta to the seat behind Daddy. He usually let me sit there. What was best, though, was the front seat, but Momma always took that when she came.

"I can already taste fried bass and mashed potatoes and cornbread and strawberry preserves and macaroni and cheese, and maybe some chocolate pie, Momma," Daddy said as we pulled into the yard.

"Got to clean these fish, Bitty Bit," he said. I ran into the kitchen to get some newspaper and a pan of cold water. I pulled Momma's big butcher knife out of the drawer, too. Then I carried everything out to the back porch to Daddy. Much as I like to eat fish, I can't stand to see them killed. So I didn't even glance at the floor when Daddy cut off their heads.

"You can look now, Bitty Bit," Daddy said. He grunted and wiped fish scales off his hands. "Lots of meat on your bass here."

"I was scared he was gonna get away," I admitted. "But I remembered that you said to hold your pole higher if you couldn't get it in, and let the fish get tired."

"Whew." He shook his head. His smile made his eyes crinkle up. "For nine years old, you sure do listen good. You're gonna be a champion fishergirl."

After Daddy finished with the fish, he let me take the pan of water with the fish fillets to the kitchen to Momma. Then I watched Daddy help Alberta tighten the brakes on her bike in the front yard.

Momma didn't take long to get dinner ready, and we didn't take long to eat it, either. Daddy wiped his mouth when he finished. "And now, how about a movie?" he asked.

"All right," Momma and Alberta said together. "Margie, you get in the bathroom first," Momma told me.

I hurried into that bathroom and splashed water everywhere. "Oh, we're going to the movies," I sang.

I guess I got carried away, because Alberta had to beat on the bathroom door. "Hurry up and get your fat behind out of there," she shouted. "I gotta use the bathroom!"

I opened the door and stuck my tongue out. She was the one who could stay in there all day staring at herself. But I finished up and got out and changed clothes. Then guess what? I had to wait and wait for everyone else to get ready.

Finally we were all set to go. We jumped in the car and headed for the Malco. We saw *Dracula and His Seven Brides*, ate candy bars, drank pop, and screamed. Course, I wasn't really scared. After the show was over, a lot of people we knew gathered around Daddy and joked with him. Everybody liked Daddy.

It was past ten o'clock when we got home. The Carson family sure partied today! The telephone rang as we came in the door, and Momma answered it. "I bet that's Miz Orange with some gossip," I said to Alberta. "I wonder if her foot's still hurting from when Ethel tromped it."

I had planned to sleep with my necklace on, but Alberta told me that the chain might break if I did. "You know how you flounce around when you sleep."

I put on clean pajamas and washed up for bed, but I wasn't sleepy. Maybe we could get Daddy and Momma to play spades or Monopoly. The telephone rang again. "Who's doing all that calling?" I asked Alberta.

When I went to the door to find out, I ran into Momma. Her mouth was turned down at the ends. "Girls, I've got bad news," she said. "Daddy has to go back to work tomorrow morning."

"Oh, phooey." Alberta banged her comb down on the dresser.

I flopped on my bed. "But he just got here!" I shouted.

"Well, one of the other drivers got sick at the last minute." Momma started to say something else, but the telephone rang again. She hurried away.

"I'm getting tired of Daddy being gone all the time," I said, fighting back tears. I never got to see Daddy as much as I wanted. This time we wouldn't even get a chance to sit out on the steps and talk. Why did he have to be an ole furniture mover anyway?

I got up, snapped off the light, and sat on my bed. I decided not to even kiss him good night. But at last I crept out and peeked into the living room. Daddy lay on the couch flexing his toes.

"C'mere, Bitty Bit," he said when he saw me, "and give me a kiss." I hung by the door and shook my head. "It won't hurt to lay one on your ole man." He made some room on the couch. "Bitty Bit scared to give her old man a hug? Guess I'll just have to cry."

To keep from smiling, I poked out my lip. Daddy never cried. I walked over to him real slow and he picked me up and hugged me. We snuggled up together on the couch for a long time. I didn't say anything and he didn't either. Just when I started to get sleepy, I remembered Ethel.

"You know that kid Ethel Hardisen?" He nodded. "She tore up Miz Silk's shop something terrible," I said, shaking my head like Momma does. "And then Momma and us had to go over to Miz Mary's trailer—"

"Your momma told me," he said. "Well, I'm glad my girls don't behave like that. Course, you both know better. Your momma raises you right." He was quiet, stroking his beard.

I began to get sleepy. I could have gone right off to sleep by Daddy, but he told me to go to bed. I gave him two hard hugs. "Daddy, how come you got to be gone so much?"

"Because I love you. I mean, a man with two beautiful girls like you and Alberta wants to do everything he can to take good care of them. So he needs a good job. Good night, baby."

I went to bed, but before I went to sleep, I whispered, "Good night, Daddy." I'd forgotten to say it to him.

Suddenly I woke up. Someone was poking me in the arm and hissing my name. From the dark came loud voices. The radio? I struggled to come all awake. "Margie? Margie!" It was Alberta. "Margie! Momma and Daddy's fighting!"

Groggy with sleep and fear, I followed Alberta to our door. We heard Daddy's heavy voice and Momma's soft voice, both at once.

"They're talking about Ethel," Alberta whispered, her ear against the crack of our door. "Daddy wants Momma to tell him why she's trying to embarrass the family." Daddy's voice bellowed over Momma's. "Daddy said something about Uncle Jake."

"Ethel? Uncle Jake?" I felt like I was still asleep. Uncle Jake, Momma's brother, was clear over in St. Louis. And why should Momma and Daddy be fighting over Ethel? I thought I was going to get sick to my stomach. I tried not to hear Daddy's loud voice clashing against Momma's soft one like a rock against a stick.

But the yelling was getting louder. It sounded like it was right outside our door. "You're always taking up with white folks!" Daddy yelled. "All the time! Always talking about doing the proper thing!" His voice was pounding. "I don't care what you say. Keep away from that woman!"

Real plain Momma cried out, "But it *is* the proper thing to do!"

A door slammed. Silence.

I ran to Alberta's bed and pulled the blanket over my head. "What are they doing now, Alberta?" I was worried to death. I'd never heard Daddy argue with Momma like this before. Alberta crept back into bed and clutched my arm.

"Margie, Daddy was fussing about Momma wanting to have Ethel come over here. About her staying with us!"

I couldn't believe what Alberta had just said. I started to cry about Momma and Daddy fighting, and then I cried harder when I remembered that Daddy would have to leave so soon. I guess I cried myself to sleep.

Breakfast was terrible. Nobody said anything until it was almost over. I chewed on my biscuit. As much as I loved biscuits, they didn't have much taste this morning. I kept my eyes down toward my plate.

"Well, girls, I hate to leave like this," Daddy said, "but a job's a job. And they'll give me more time when I come back home. They better."

When Daddy tried to talk to Alberta, she only mumbled at him. He didn't say a word to Momma and she didn't say a word to him.

Out of the corner of my eye I saw Alberta put down her fork. "Is Ethel coming over here?" she asked suddenly.

"Yes," said Momma.

"No," said Daddy. They looked real mean at each other. "I told you, Luvenia, don't bring that girl into my house."

I dropped my biscuit and looked at Daddy. "Why would she have to come here?" My voice squeaked.

"Because Miz Mary has to go away to get some money and some help," Momma said. "And she can't take Ethel with her and there's no one else to take care of her."

Alberta scowled. "I don't want that ole funky girl around me. She belongs with Miz Mary."

"Don't you bring that kid in here, and that's final," Daddy said. He glared at Momma, and Momma glared back.

At first I thought they were going to start arguing. "Are you-all gonna fight again?" I whispered.

Momma and Daddy looked at me sharp. Then they both looked real sad. Finally Daddy cleared his throat and got up from the table. "I've got to go. Give me kisses, ladies."

Alberta and I pushed back our chairs slowly. I always hated this part, having to watch him leave. I wrapped my arms around his neck and hugged him as hard as I could. My tears smeared on his beard.

Daddy whispered, "It won't be long, Bitty Bit, it won't be long. Now you be good for me, okay?" He hugged Alberta, who was crying, too. "Don't give your momma a hard time about the boys, Alberta," he told her, "especially if his name is Billy Ray Morgan."

We all walked to the front porch. Daddy put his foot on the step, hesitated, turned around, and looked at Momma. They stared at each other, and then Momma flew across the porch and embraced him. That set us off to crying again. When they finally let loose of each other, Daddy got into the car.

"Your suitcase, Matt!" Momma ran back into the house. She handed him his old battered green suitcase.

Daddy started up the car and waved at us. "Now you take good care of each other and your momma," he shouted. Then he was gone.

We watched until we couldn't see the car. Alberta and I went back into our room and lay down. I felt so low. There was so much I'd wanted to tell him. I felt all ready to burst open. Where was that old plumber's hammer he said I could use to build a scooter? He had promised on his last trip home that he would even help me build it. And I needed his permission to beat up Missy Walker, a girl Alberta's age who'd been giving me a hard time. Momma always said no right off to these kinds of things, but Daddy listened first.

"Out of bed, girls," said Momma as she came into our room. "Ethel is coming tonight. She'll go back home tomorrow evening. It's just for the weekend. So get up; we've got lots to do."

I sat up like a shot. "But Daddy said she couldn't come!"

Alberta's mouth gaped open. "Momma, Daddy said—"

"I am aware of what your father said." Momma folded her arms across her chest. "I've told you once that Ethel is coming tonight, and I don't plan to have to say it again."

Alberta rolled her eyes. "Oh shoot! I sure can't have anybody over with *her* here!"

I was mad, too. "Where's she gonna sleep?"

Momma unfolded her arms and slipped her hands in

the pockets of her yellow robe. "How about with you?"

"Me? Unh-unh, Momma, not in my bed, please!"

"Why not? Ethel's not—"

"I don't want her in my bed!" I jumped up and thrashed my arms around.

"You look like a monkey, Margie," Momma snapped. "Please stop."

"Momma, couldn't you put her on the couch?" Alberta pleaded. "She don't have to be in here with us."

"Alberta, you do know how to speak English correctly. Girls, Ethel's just a little girl. She's not going to give us germs or rob us. We'll eat dinner tonight, maybe go to the movies, and tomorrow we'll all go to church."

"Church?" Alberta wailed. "Take her to church with us?"

"I don't want her in my bed!"

"I've said all that I'm going to say," Momma warned. "If I can stand it, so can you."

I wrung my hands, pulled my braids, poked out my lips, and stamped my feet. Alberta just groaned. I turned to her after Momma walked out. "What are we gonna do?"

"Girl, I don't know, but it doesn't look like much."

"I wish Daddy was here," I said.

"You and me both."

Momma had us cleaning and scrubbing and dusting the whole house. I even had to put clean sheets on my bed. "My poor sheets," I fussed, patting them. "They got to have that dirty ole thing rolling around on them."

That day went so fast. When it started to get dark, I went outside to my peach tree and sat under it. Usually I liked twilight, but I sure didn't this time. Twilight meant nighttime and nighttime meant Ethel. Tomorrow at church Missy and Sarah and everybody would laugh and gossip about Miz Carson and her daughters taking in trash. And tonight that kid would bite and kick and cuss me and stick her finger up in my face. Oh!

If Ethel were clean and nice and regular white, or clean and nice and regular Black—or just plain nice—folks would say, "Ain't it sweet about Miz Carson keeping Miz Mary's girl?" They sure wouldn't say that the way she was now!

"Margie, get ready for supper!" There went Alberta like the voice of doom. I pressed closer to my peach tree and waited. After a few minutes Alberta trotted down the path. I hoped she wouldn't see me. Of course she wasn't blind, so she did.

"You're hunched up against that tree like a big, fat weed," she said.

"I ain't fat." I liked to say ain't when Momma wasn't around. "Why does Momma have to keep that ole girl?"

Alberta let out an irritated sigh. "You've been asking me that all day, and I keep telling you the same thing. You got nerve, anyway, to be so upset. You're not the only one's gonna suffer."

"She ain't got to sleep in your bed!" I shot back.

"And you just keep her over there with you, too," said Alberta. "Now, come on in."

Our gray-shingled one-story house fit only Daddy and Momma and Alberta and me—there was no place in it for Ethel. She would just mess everything up, but there wasn't anything I could do about it. I sat there as long as I dared, hoping Alberta would say that Momma was really joking about Ethel coming over. But she didn't, so I turned down my mouth and hauled myself up.

3

Momma was cooking cornbread, kidney beans, rice, and fried chicken when I came into the kitchen. I nearly burned up. She had the fan on the floor trying to blow the heat out through the window. "Do you think you can wash that chocolate-bar look off your face?" she asked as she pushed her hair back from her face.

I slouched into the bathroom and splashed water on my face. What did I care that my face looked like a square chocolate bar? That's how Momma said it looked whenever I got mad. Well, I just clamped down on my back teeth and made my jaw muscles stick out more. I was that disgusted. As soon as I came back out, the doorbell rang. My stomach jumped.

"Well, here you are," said Momma. I kind of slid my eyes toward the front door. Miz Mary was yakking already, about how something smelled good. They came into the kitchen and right away Ethel started jumping around. Same ole dirty face. Same dirty hands. Dirty red shirt and too-big sandals that flopped when she walked. She climbed onto a kitchen chair, jerking at the tablecloth, and one of Momma's best plates shattered on the floor.

"Don't do that, Ethel," said Miz Mary real low. She looked at Momma and back at the plate. We could all see that the plate was broken, but still she had to say, "Oh, it broke."

"Take somebody a million years to glue that back together," I said.

But Momma shrugged. "Everything's all right. It's just one of my old plates, anyway."

Only Momma could think up something like that to say to guests when an accident happened. Alberta got out of her chair to get the broom, and I was left alone at the table with Ethel. She opened her mouth wide, stuck her forefinger in her right nostril, and pushed her tongue out at me.

"You better stop," I warned her.

"Behave, Margie," said Momma.

Well, I fell back in my chair. Why was Momma getting after me?

Miz Mary lit a cigarette and watched Alberta sweep up pieces of plate. Ashes from her cigarette floated down on the table. "I'd sure like to stay and eat, but the bus leaves in fifteen minutes. I got just enough time to walk to the depot."

She handed Momma a T-shirt, a pair of raggedy underwear, a pair of faded red shorts, and a pair of gray socks that looked like they should have been white. Ethel's clothes reminded me of the old stuff Momma donated to the people at the poor farm.

"She better be good." Miz Mary cut her eyes at Ethel. "If I find out you ain't been good I'll beat you till you don't know which end is up!"

Miz Mary walked away and Ethel began to whimper. I was getting to feel sorry for her, but then that kid started to scream. Miz Mary didn't even have to hear it. By that time she was out the door and gone.

"Hush, hush, your momma's going away for just a little while," Momma explained to Ethel. "She'll be back tomorrow night. Everything will be really nice for you here. You and I and the girls will have lots of fun."

"Humph," Alberta said real low.

"First I'm going to wash your face, honey." Momma walked to the bathroom and got a cloth. But as soon as she came toward Ethel, that humdinger zipped around the living room screaming like she was crazy.

Momma was able to swipe at Ethel's face a couple

of times after she trapped her in the corner. Then she came back to the table and coaxed Ethel over with a chicken leg.

"Let's eat our dinner, dear," Momma said. Ethel bit off a huge chunk of chicken and threw the rest of it on the floor. Then she squished the rice with her fingers. "Don't play with your food, Ethel." Momma's voice was low and she did not change the expression on her face, but I thought I was going to be sick.

Suddenly Ethel leaped from the table and sprayed a mouthful of beans and rice onto the living-room carpet.

"Boy, this is gonna be some weekend," I said.

Well, I picked up the chicken bone, and then followed everybody into the living room. I watched Alberta sweep up the beans. A few minutes ago she'd been sweeping up pieces of bowl. I waited for Momma to jump on Ethel this time, but instead she just pulled her into the bathroom. Ethel was yowling and Momma was ignoring it. "Isn't it nice to have a clean face? Let me put some fresh clothes on you, Ethel. Ethel!"

A few minutes later Momma came out of the bathroom patting her Afro. "Margie! Would you please take your fingers out of your ears? Don't be evil."

Well, I felt evil.

Momma helped Alberta finish cleaning up the carpet, and kept an eye on Ethel. So did I. I didn't know what that kid was going to do next.

"Would you like to see a movie?" Momma asked us.

"Yeah, *Dragonfly* is playing at the Malco," I yelled.

"Oh, good," Momma said. "Let's get ready."

I ran to our room, eagerly strapped on my new sandals, and pulled on my white, frilly, halter top and my new green shorts. When I returned, Alberta was complaining to Momma. "But Ethel hasn't been behaving, so why should she behave at the show?"

"Don't wanna go to no show!" Ethel said. I looked at her and saw Momma had tied one of my red ribbons around her dirty hair.

My mouth was open, ready to break out at this, but I couldn't get a word in.

"Ethel will do all right," Momma said to Alberta, "if we're just patient."

Alberta put her hands on her hips. "I don't care to go."

Momma paused from straightening Ethel's shorts. "Yes, you do. And I don't care to hear another word."

Alberta was just afraid that Billy Ray Morgan would be at the movies with that ole white towel slung over his skinny shoulder. She didn't want him to see her with Ethel. Momma always said Billy Ray looked like a fool with his hair in braids and that "Afro Now" T-shirt cut off high on his belly. But to me he just looked like some big ole skinny boy.

Then I got to thinking. I didn't want anybody to see me with Ethel either, but it was too late now. When we got to the door, Alberta pointed to Ethel. "You take her hand," she ordered.

"Me? You! You're the oldest."

"You better, else I'll put a knot on your head!" She motioned at me, but I stayed where I was while Momma walked on out the door with Ethel.

"You think many kids'll see us?" I asked Alberta.

"Probably," she fumed, "and it's all your fault, big mouth." She wore her new straw wedgies and her feet were going every which way. So was her head, swiveling left and right trying to catch someone out staring at us.

"It's not my fault," I said.

"You're the one wanted to go. You had to holler out first."

"Well, what are we gonna do?"

"Since you're the one who wanted to go, just shut up and watch the movie," she snapped. "And hold Ethel on your lap and feed her popcorn."

We got to town quicker than usual. It wasn't that hot outside, but I was sweating, I guess because Ethel was with us. In front of her house Miz Ludwig was watering her azaleas and petunias. I noticed that a lot of people were outside for early evening, but at least they were busy and not just sitting on their porches.

Mr. Cranshaw's truck stand was open in the First Baptist Church parking lot. He sold okra, peas, corn, and watermelons. He was sitting by his truck with his hands in the pockets of his faded green bib apron when we came up. "Evenin', Miz Carson." He leaned his slat-bottom chair back on its hind legs. I could hear money jingling in his apron pockets.

"Evening," Momma said. "Do you expect to have some honeydew melons pretty soon?"

"Might." He stopped jingling to rub his thick red nose with a long, red finger. "Who you got there?"

"This is Ethel Hardisen, just an overnight guest."

Ethel stuck out her tongue. "Don't like you," she said, screwing up her mouth. Momma gasped and pulled her up the sidewalk. Mr. Cranshaw just blinked and set his chair down with a clunk.

Ahead of us the neon lights of the Malco flickered brighter and brighter. People were lined up outside waiting to buy tickets. One of them was that loud-mouthed, gold-toothed, hateful Missy Walker. "Oh, Alberta, Margie, hey Ethel!" she screamed.

Everybody waiting in line turned and looked at us. So we had to walk half a block in front of all those eyes. I thought I would have a stroke. When we got in line, Ethel balled up her fist at everybody and snarled.

"Ethel, for heavens' sakes!" Momma hissed. "Stop this nonsense!"

Everybody saw that, too. "Momma, please, please make her behave," Alberta said through barely moving lips.

Well, we finally got inside. As soon as the movie started, Ethel shouted, "Don't like no dragon!" and fought Momma, who was trying to hold her on her lap. When Momma told her to hush, Ethel slapped at her.

I really wanted to get my hands around that brat's neck for trying to hit my mother.

"What's the matter with that kid?" I heard somebody behind us say. I scrouched down in my seat and acted like I didn't know who sat beside me.

I noticed that Ethel got real quiet after a while. She was so still, I couldn't concentrate on the movie, but when I finally did, do you know what happened? Off she jumped down the aisle!

"Come back here!" Momma cried.

"Momma, I told you!" Alberta said.

Ethel got all the way to the first row. She started to dance and make funny shapes on the screen, blotting out what was going on. Three ushers hurried toward her, but she scampered off to the other side of the theater. An usher ran up the aisle and cut off her route, another one closed in on her, and a third dragged her back to Momma while she screamed and kicked. Even they knew who she was with.

"Tie this kid down," said one of the ushers.

Momma took Ethel by both wrists and settled her back on her lap. She wrapped her arms around Ethel's waist and held her feet with her legs. "Don't you bite me," Momma warned.

Ethel shrieked, "Lemme go!"

People around us began to mumble and complain. When Momma turned around to speak to them, Ethel slipped off her lap and ran all over the place. "Let's boogie, baby, umph, umph, umph," she sang, snapping her fingers and sticking out her behind.

The ushers had to run her down again. "This kid kick

me one more time, I'm gonna kick her back," said one as he pushed Ethel back to Momma.

In a few minutes Mr. Streit, the manager, came up. "Ma'am, don't you think you ought to take her home?"

Momma chewed on her lip. Then she looked over at us. "Girls, we'd better go."

"But, Momma," Alberta whispered, "why can't we watch the show? We ain't done nothin'."

I don't know which made Momma madder—having Alberta be sassy or hearing her use bad English. Momma snatched up Ethel and jerked her thumb at us. When we slunk out the doors, it seemed like the whole theater applauded.

"We can't do a doggone thing!" I told Alberta as we straggled back down the street. It wasn't even dark yet.

"We won't have any fun after she goes back to Miz Mary, either." Alberta wasn't bothering to walk sexy anymore. "People'll talk about this for months. I wouldn't be surprised to see it in the newspaper. 'Brat Upsets Theater.' That'd be the headline. And then they'll write, 'Carson Girls Blamed for Near Riot.'"

Boy, was I glad when we got home. Alberta and I went to our room. "Let's play some Monopoly," I suggested. "Want to?" But I hadn't even counted out the money good before Momma came in and said we ought to teach Ethel to play. Instead, we decided to put up the game, and that made Momma mad.

"Then I'm sure that you don't want to watch television, either," she said, frowning.

I really wanted to go outside, but I didn't want Ethel with me, so I read a book. When Momma came in again, she looked at our Big Ben clock on the dresser. "It's after nine," she said. "Since you girls have nothing else to do, you might as well go to bed."

"Go to bed? Momma!" My face crumpled.

"Margie, put on your pajamas," she said.

Momma's mood was so bad that I figured I better not mess with her. I couldn't see any way out of having to go to bed and share it with that brat, though. "You sleep on this side," I told Ethel. "But don't you dare pee."

"Watch your language, Margie Carson," Momma warned. She kneeled by Ethel and tried to hug her. "Ethel won't make water in the bed, will she?"

From the way Alberta's mouth twitched I knew she wanted to laugh, but Momma's words weren't funny to me. Ethel balled up her fist at Momma. "Ain't sleepy and I ain't gonna sleep!" she yelled.

Momma straightened Ethel's fist back into five fingers. "We don't fight around here, honey," she said. She paused, and then added, "And we don't say 'ain't.'" She took Ethel into the bathroom and after ten minutes' worth of struggle brought her out. I nearly fell over. Ethel was wearing my pajamas!

"Those are mine!"

"Ethel won't hurt your pajamas. Plus, they're dirty, anyway. Now behave, Margie."

What could I say? I stuck out my lips and clamped down on my jaw muscles and stamped my foot a couple of times while Momma's back was turned. Then I gave up and crawled into my side of the bed and lay way over at the edge. I could feel the mattress slope a little toward the other side when Ethel got in.

Momma kissed Alberta and me, but when she came over to kiss Ethel, that humdinger pulled my sheet over her head. Momma snatched back the sheet, pecked Ethel's cheek, and laughed when Ethel wiped her face.

When she left our room, everything was quiet. Ethel lay in my bed as still as a stone, but I was lying there waiting. She started to move around, and sure enough she pulled a trick. I felt my left thigh grow warm and damp.

"Momma!" I rolled out of bed, hitting my feet hard on the floor so Momma would hear. "Momma! She did it, she did it! She peed in my bed!"

Momma came in and snapped on the lights. Part of her hair was braided and part was still Afro. She looked around and then she said to me, "If you use that word again, Margie, I shall spank you."

My eyes went wide. "But, Momma, she—"

"Ethel, you have the bed to yourself now."

Momma said it like she was praising that ole girl. "Margie, sleep with your sister, please."

Alberta flashed her eyes at us. "I don't know why I got to get dragged into this," she fumed. When Momma lifted her hand, though, Alberta backed down. "You gotta change your pajamas," she said real quick to me. "I don't want my bed all smelly."

I was still so surprised over Momma's threat that I couldn't say a word. I put on some more pajamas, got in Alberta's bed, and tried to find room.

"You better not scratch me with your ole toenails," said Alberta.

"Don't you be scratching me, either. And quit pushing."

Momma brought in one of Daddy's old shirts, pulled Ethel out of my sopping pajamas, and slipped on the shirt. "Sleep on Margie's side," she told her.

Off went the lights again. When I thought it was safe, I whispered to Alberta, "It wasn't my fault, but see? Momma didn't even get mad at Ethel!"

"You don't get mad at overnight guests," Alberta said, "so since Ethel's a guest in your bed, don't you get mad, either. You ought to be there entertaining her."

We lay there. My jaw muscles were as tight as the lock on our front door. Everyone was sleeping in their own beds but Ethel and me, and Ethel didn't count. Some overnight guest.

The next morning I woke up to water splashing. Momma was saying, "Sit still." It sounded like elbows and knees were hitting the bathtub. Yowling and shrieking and bawling and screeching.

I woke up all the way, and everything came back to me: Ethel! I bet she slept with Momma, too, because I woke up off and on all night and she never was in our room.

"Lay still," mumbled Alberta. "You made noises all night."

"I was cold. You didn't give me any covers. Listen! Ethel's acting up again. I bet that girl even slept with Momma!"

"You don't know that," Alberta said.

"Yes, I do." Alberta was always trying to act like she was smarter than me.

"You know, she coulda slept on the couch." She yawned. "I bet Momma's trying to clean her up. I hope I don't have to clean out the tub. I'd be scrubbing off dirt for days."

Alberta squinted at me and I squinted back. Without saying a word to each other, we tiptoed out of our room to the open bathroom door. Momma was on her knees beside the tub and Ethel was in it. Momma had both of Ethel's wrists in one of her hands and was scrubbing skin with the other. Even though Ethel was shouting and kicking water all over the place, Momma was washing the devil out of her.

"You may kick and scream," Momma tried to sing, "but you're gonna get clean." The front of her robe was wet. She wrung out the cloth, but when she set down the Ivory soap Ethel flung it against the cabinet mirror. Pieces of soap clung to the mirror and the rest thunked into the basin.

"Oh no, you don't!" Momma pulled another bar out of her robe pocket quick as a flash and kept on scrubbing without missing a lick. Ethel slipped down in the tub and grabbed a handful of Momma's braids trying to get up. Alberta and I almost died trying not to laugh.

The next thing we knew, Momma had jammed the washcloth in Ethel's mouth!

"Phhhfh!" Ethel sputtered. I slapped my hand over my mouth so nobody could hear me laugh. Momma had put a washcloth in my mouth once. Why, I don't remember, but you can believe I hadn't done whatever it was since.

"When I take this washrag out, I hope you won't start that noise again," Momma scolded that kid. "You sound like a tomcat yowling on a fence." Then her voice got soft and she began to talk like she was teaching in her classroom. "You're a little girl, so if you want to pretend that you're a cat just say 'Meow.' Plus you're driving me crazy."

Ethel was still frowned up, but she kept quiet. "Good girl!" Momma said, smiling. One of her braids had unraveled, and water drops were all over her hair. If her hair had been pressed like she used to do it a couple of years ago, it would have turned back to frizziness. "Now let's get dried off and get some talcum powder on so you can smell good."

We tiptoed back to our room and sat down on Alberta's bed. In case Momma asked, we decided to tell her that we thought the tub had overflowed and we wanted to check. But I don't think she saw us.

"Did Ethel sleep with you?" I asked Momma at breakfast.

She nodded. "And did I see you screw up your face just now?" She made a face back at me, then laughed. She knew I couldn't stand to be laughed at! "Margie Carson, you jealous thing. Do you want me to give you a bath, too?"

"Alberta saw, too!" I was hot. Why did she have to tease me?

Ethel didn't say a word during breakfast. I noticed, too, that she ate her cereal and toast and drank her juice without spilling, spitting, or throwing a crumb. I figured she planned to save her energy for later. And I knew where later would be: church!

We cleared the table and Alberta declared that she would wash the dishes, which meant that she wouldn't have to dry them or sweep the floor. I guess she thought she had used that broom enough last night. I wiped the dishes dry as slowly as I could.

"You're just stalling," said Alberta, "'cause you think you can stall your way out of going to church. Momma's gonna come in here and get after you." She dropped the knives in the rinse water, and splashes hit the wallpaper and the floor. "You better not let Ethel wet your bed again, either, 'cause you're not gonna sleep with me anymore."

"Ethel'll be gone tonight anyway, so there." I switched my behind at her, then quickly sneaked a glance toward the door. "What do you think Daddy would do if he knew that Ethel was gonna go to church with us?"

"Ask Momma."

"No, you ask."

When Momma stopped by the kitchen, Alberta shot me a meaningful look, but I kept my mouth shut. "Better hurry up, girls" was all Momma said.

I dried a little faster until she left the room. Then out of the blue, Alberta said, "I hope Billy Ray's not at church this morning."

Mooning again over that boy! I was tired of Billy Ray, Billy Ray, Billy Ray. "I know all about it," I said. "I've seen you, just sighing at yourself and staring in the mirror and playing with your hair." I giggled as she got mad. "Ain't fooled nobody."

Alberta flung down the washcloth and glared at me. The two spots on her cheeks were red. Then she suddenly stared past me. I turned around to see what she was looking at and got the shock of my life.

Ethel had on my yellow dress!

"Fits just right, doesn't it?" Momma said. "I had to work it over quite a bit, I'll tell you that. Ethel, you look so pretty! Turn around for Margie."

That used to be my favorite dress. When Momma had sewed it, she had added delicate ruffles and shell buttons and tiny pockets for my Sunday school money. "Momma, she can't wear that!" I cried. I didn't care if it was old-fashioned and too small for me. It was mine!

"Oh, yes, she can," Momma said firmly. "Everybody liked it when you wore it, so they ought to like Ethel wearing it. Besides, Miz Mary didn't leave any dresses for Ethel. I'm surprised at the way you've been acting. I thought you liked to share."

Ethel hopped around. She held her arms straight like a ballerina and her hair flounced in yellowish-red ringlets. Those ole floppy sandals were white and so were her socks. But she still looked ugly to me. Momma was carrying on like Ethel was some princess or a movie star. Maybe if I had that hair and tore up stuff Momma would make a fuss over me, too. I slammed the spatula I was holding down on the table and threw the dish towel in the drawer.

"Girl, look what you're doing." Alberta had to add her little smart remarks too. "You're just jealous because Momma pays attention to Ethel."

"I am not. You keep teasing and I'll tell Billy Ray you're on your period!" I charged off to our room and fell on Alberta's bed. I could still smell that ole Ethel's pee. She'd lit up the whole room.

Alberta came in right behind me. "You better stop talking about Billy Ray or else I'll blast you one. And get off my bed."

Since I was mad, too, I stayed where I was. Alberta wrenched my arm, doubled up her fist, and hit me on the thigh, but I smacked her right back—in the nose. We tangled on the bed, all wrapped up in the sheets and blankets. Alberta rolled over on me and I thought she was going to smother me with her big ole skinny self.

"What in the world?" Momma flew in, took one look

and snatched us apart. "I've had enough of this, Margie! *Your* pajamas, *your* ribbon, *your* bed, *your* dress—your attitude has been very nasty about everything all weekend. Why, that dress doesn't even fit you."

I began to cry and tears dripped off my chin. "But it's mine!"

"And now it belongs to Ethel, understand? I said, do you understand?"

"Y-y-yes, ma'am."

"Now get in that bathroom and take your bath. And if I have to get after you one more time, take your soul to Jesus, little girl."

As Momma left the room her bare feet smacked loudly on the wood floor. Alberta glanced at me from where she had tried to hide by the closet. "Yeah, you better do what she says, 'cause if you don't, your little fat behind's gonna belong to Momma."

I just stared at the ceiling. The morning wasn't even half over. I started to feel real bad, but I made myself remember that Momma could always wash my clothes and my sheets. By tonight, anyway, that Ethel would be gone.

4

In Nutbrush people like to get good looks at anything that is even a little bit strange. Like if somebody's dog gets loose or somebody gets a new car, everyone in town will slow down and gawk. So you know they had a party with us. There was Momma high-stepping out in front, dragging Ethel all fancied up in *my* dress, and Alberta and me slouching behind. And it looked like just about everybody had got out on their front porches in time to eyeball us going by.

"Come along, girls!" Momma said sweetly. "Oh, isn't this a lovely day? Good morning, good morning."

"I wish she'd be quiet and just walk on up the street," Alberta groaned. "My life is ruined."

Alberta had a lot of nerve. She was just worried about Billy Ray. Didn't she realize that my life was ruined, too?

It seemed like we hit the church in two minutes. Missy, Sarah, and Billy Ray were standing in the grass next to the church parking lot. "Oh, there he is," Alberta said, patting her Afro and trying to strut in her sandals.

"Hello," said Momma pleasantly to Missy and Sarah. She didn't speak to Billy Ray, but he was the only one who answered her. He looked his regular sleepy-eyed self, but at least he'd taken down his braids and left his towel at home.

We had just got down the stairs and into the basement when I heard Sarah behind us say, "That girl's got on Margie's dress!"

I whirled around. "So?" I shouted. "I gave it to her!"

"Margie!" said Momma, putting her hand to her mouth.

In the basement everybody had frozen still to stare at Ethel, even the old folks. All those eyes! Probably remembering how Ethel had squashed her foot, Miz Orange moved way back from her. Dr. Sage, who had been a college professor in the old days, had to close his Bible to take a good look at Ethel. And Bennie Ball, a fat three-year-old who looked just like his name, got widemouthed as he stood there. I bet he remembered that time when Ethel picked her nose and smeared that finger on his arm.

Momma walked on in smiling. "Hello, hello," she was saying like she'd had Ethel with us for years. She led her to the primary class, which she taught. I saw the little kids playing around their table get quiet and still. They didn't do that because of Momma; they did it because of Ethel. I bet every one of those kids had been smacked or chewed on by Ethel at least once.

"I hope nobody starts any more stuff," I said as Alberta and I sat down at the intermediate class table. Missy and Sarah switched in through the door. I was worried they would start something and I didn't know what I could do, but luckily our teacher, Miz Hamlin, was right behind them. For once I was glad she was strict on church behavior. Maybe she would keep those girls from teasing me.

But when Miz Hamlin sat her big behind in the chair next to me, I groaned. Who wanted to sit by the teacher? Over in the corner I could hear Momma's class quacking like a flock of ducklings. Except for one ole chicken: Ethel! She was snuggled up against Momma, not saying a word. But she didn't fool me.

"Ethel'll start acting up. You watch," I whispered too loud to Alberta. "Everybody knows she's just waiting for Sunday school to start."

When Miz Hamlin talks, she sounds like her dog Buster. Ferocious! "No whispering, Margie," she growled. "We are in the house of the Lord."

Well, Sunday school started. First Missy rubbed her nose, but it looked like she was doing it at me and Alberta. She threw her eyes over at Momma's class, back at me, and then she turned her head real slow and stared at Sarah. Sarah acted like she was gonna die trying not to laugh. Miz Hamlin, though, didn't say a word. I kicked at Missy, missed, then scrunched down in my chair and kicked at her again.

"Margaret Carson," Miz Hamlin said, "read the next verse."

"Genesis, chapter five, verse one," I stammered. "'This is the book of the generations—'"

"No! Not paying attention is disrespect to the Lord."

"Genesis, chapter four, verse twenty-three," I read. "'And Lamech said—'"

"No!" Miz Hamlin's hand slammed on the table, and I jumped. "Disrespect for the Lord can send your soul to hell, Margaret, and sure get you in deep with me."

I was so embarrassed. And when I side-eyed a glance over at Momma, I could tell she had seen and heard what happened too. Ethel had her ole nasty hand in the crook of Momma's elbow. I felt all by myself.

"It's Genesis, chapter four, verse thirteen," Alberta whispered.

"Alberta Joyce Carson! Whispering! Read, Melissa!"

"Genesis, chapter four, verse thirteen," lisped Missy.

"'And Cain said unto the Lord, My punishment is greater than I can bear.'" She grinned and her ole gold tooth sparkled when she made a face at me.

"Read this verse, Johnny! Read that verse, Robert! Read that verse, William!" Miz Hamlin commanded. She went around the table a million times until everybody started to give me evil looks.

When Miz Hamlin asked us to close our eyes for prayer, I shut mine just enough to let through a ray of sight and discovered that Sarah and Missy were wrinkling up their noses at me. Nervy! Even Ambrose, who I kinda liked, was looking at me sourly. I wished Gloria Hinkle was here. She was my friend most of the time and maybe she would have taken up for me. And where was Lizzie Carlton? She should have been here. The roads were dry today. See, she lived way out in the country and if it rained the roads would get so bad she couldn't get in.

Miz Hamlin was still praying when the other classes ended. She always had a long prayer. When she finally finished, I could feel her eyes on me. I picked up a hymn book quickly and with the rest of the Sunday school sang "Onward, Christian Soldiers." As soon as our superintendent, Mr. Crook, whispered his last amen, I pushed back my chair, but a cold, wrinkled hand clamped itself on my arm.

"You stay," Miz Hamlin said. "Now we're going to concentrate on our lessons next Sunday! Aren't we?"

"Yes, ma'am." I knew the other kids were listening.

"And we will sit still! Won't we?"

"Yes, ma'am." If she kept this up, I wouldn't get any free time before choir. The junior choir always met upstairs after Sunday school to go over our songs for church service. But the worst part was that Momma was standing right there and heard every word Miz Hamlin said to me.

"What did you learn this morning?"

"I learned about Cain."

"What did you learn about Cain?"

"That he didn't want to be punished," I answered. Momma went past slowly, still catching every word. That ole Ethel was holding on hard to her hand, too.

Ethel! Wearing my yellow dress and making everyone tease me. Ethel hugging up around Momma in Sunday school. Making me get in trouble with Miz Hamlin!

"The Lord punished Cain! Cain killed his brother!" Miz Hamlin shoved her forefinger in the air like our pastor did when he got the spirit. "You should mend your erring ways because the Lord knows everything you say, everything you do and everything you think! You can go!"

If Miz Hamlin was right, then the Lord also knew I had almost kicked Missy and wished I could have snatched that Ethel away from my momma and run her on back to her ole raggedy trailer! To keep from crying, I rushed to the rest room and washed my face.

The piano upstairs began to plunk out "Amazing Grace," which was the signal for choir to assemble. I could imagine Miz Wilkins's crooked, fat fingers bouncing over the keys. When I peeked out the rest-room door and didn't see anyone, I ran up the wooden stairs so I wouldn't have to hang around the other kids and be teased about getting bawled out.

"How's your guest?" Miz Wilkins asked as I sat down in the choir box.

"Unh-hunh." How could I answer a question like that?

"Beg pardon?"

"Fine, ma'am," I said through my teeth.

"Your momma tells me that Ethel's mother is supposed to come back tonight, but I wonder." She rolled her fingers up to the high keys and hit a wrong note. Everybody was used to that, though. Miz Wilkins had never taken piano lessons. "Don't you remember when that woman left Ethel overnight, it was supposed to be, with the Swensens? Didn't come back for ten days!"

Miz Wilkins wasn't fooling me. She was just trying to pick some gossip. People were always picking gossip from children, asking things they knew not to ask folks their own age. Momma always warned me to keep our family business to ourselves. So I just said, "Oh," and looked in my hymn book.

But Miz Wilkins wouldn't let up. She got to scaring me with what happened to the Swensens, an old white couple who ran Swensen's Dry Cleaners and Laundry. "They took that child in out of the kindness of their hearts," she said gravely. "They're Jehovah's Witnesses, you know. Well, Ethel's momma was gone so long and Ethel was so bad, they finally had to send her to that Children's Home."

I wanted to tell Miz Wilkins that Miz Mary would come back tonight, no doubt about it. Maybe those Swensens misunderstood about how long Miz Mary was supposed to be gone. I heard feet on the stairs. Alberta walked up with Billy Ray slouching behind her. Then came Sandy, Sarah, Missy, Donald, Esther, Evelyn, all of them. Chattering and laughing, they sat down around me.

"Doesn't Ethel look cute this morning?" That was Angeline!

"Couldn't nobody look as pretty as Ethel with that dress on," said Missy.

Instead of soprano, I wished that I sang tenor or bass. Then I'd be in the back row and Miz Wilkins wouldn't have been able to see me kick Angeline's heel and whop Missy in the head for being so nasty.

"You tease my sister one more time, Missy, and I'll mash your face in," Alberta said.

I threw a grateful grin over at her. Just then Miz Wilkins clapped her hands for silence and told us the lineup of songs.

Mr. Crook sat down in the front pew next to the aisle. Besides being in charge of the Sunday school, he was also head deacon and always sat in the same spot, no matter what. Members of the congregation began to straggle in. Like two old elm trees bending in the wind, Mr. and Mrs. Forrester swayed down the aisle. Miz Bessie Boston, who always gave thanks to the Lord for curing her nosebleeds, limped along behind them.

It was past time for church to start. I wondered when Momma would come up. But as soon as I saw her climbing up the stairs with Ethel, my palms got wet. People peeked their heads around to get good looks at Ethel. A few whispered to each other. "When I get old," I promised myself, "I'm never going to peek and poke around in church."

"Sit up, girl!" Alberta's foot cracked against my chair.

"Ethel's being better than Margie, hunh, Missy?" Sarah whispered real loud. When I heard that, tears filled my eyes. Everybody was being unfair.

Looking at us meaningfully, Miz Wilkins pounded out the introduction. We got up and sang, "Amazing Grace, How Sweet the Sound." Our voices filled the whole church. Nubia Missionary Baptist Church's junior choir could sing! It sure felt good!

But the Reverend Mr. Princey preached so long! He talked about the whole Bible. Jesus and the lepers. Jesus and the bad folks. Then he got off on John the Baptist. Finally he slowed down, wiped his face, and let us sing some more. My legs were numb from so much sitting. I was glad that church was almost over. All that was left was the testifying. I couldn't stand to keep watching that Ethel make folks think she was so good. Everybody knew she was a humdinger. Why wouldn't she act like how she really was?

Miz Orange stood up to testify. "Lord knows I'm a widow and I'm deprived, but I'm not complaining, because my way is easier now." I had heard folks say Mr. Orange used to stay out late at night and gamble and get drunk. Miz Orange didn't testify to that. But she wasn't done. "The Lord took ten pounds off me last week."

Miz Orange, I prayed, sit down!

"If Miz Orange lay off them doughnuts she'd lost ten more," Billy Ray said, and he didn't even bother to whisper.

Finally! Church was over. I hurried from the choir box over to Momma, but Miz Orange had already cornered her and was talking up a breeze. "Luvenia," she said, "how you know for sure that chile's momma is gonna come back tonight?"

Right away my stomach got to jumping from remembering what Miz Wilkins had said about the Swensens.

"Oh, I'm sure—"

"I'm not asking to be nosy," Miz Orange went on. "I'm asking for your own good and 'cause I'm your friend. I know you mean well and I know you a good Christian woman, but I sure know, too, that you don't have to go overboard. You got your own babies to feed and think about."

Instead of minding their own business, everybody stood around and listened. "I'll call you when I get home," said Momma. When she got away from Miz Orange she almost ran down old Miz Boston, who was smiling at Ethel.

"And how are you, young lady?" asked Miz Boston.

"Say, 'Fine, thank you,'" said Momma. Sweat sat like a row of ants along her nose.

Ethel stared up at Miz Boston. "You got any beer?" she asked.

Momma turned on her heels and dragged Ethel down the stairs. We hurried to catch up.

"Ethel sure was quiet," said Alberta when we got outside. "And she sat so still through everything." Of course she was pretending she didn't see Billy Ray back there in the parking lot.

With her forefinger Momma wiped the sweat off her nose. "Well," she said, "since Ethel was so good, I'm going to buy her an ice-cream cone. I promised her I would if she was quiet in church."

"What?" I nearly fell over in disbelief. "But Momma—"

"Don't you think she was a good girl?" Momma had that look in her eyes that said don't talk back. "I hardly had to hush her."

"I get some ice *cream!*" Ethel sang, dancing around, snapping her fingers, and sticking out her behind.

Even Alberta couldn't let that pass. "Don't I get some ice cream, too? You didn't have to tell me to hush."

"Of course," Momma said quickly. "But I *expect* you girls to behave, don't I, Margie?"

I figured that was her way of reminding me about that bawling out I got from Miz Hamlin. "Yes, ma'am," I said real low, but I was mad when I said it. Now that I knew why Ethel had been so phony, I decided that as soon as I got a chance I'd fix that trashy kid good.

The sun splattered around us through the oak trees as we walked down Main Street. When we went past the park I almost wanted to stop and play in the swings. At one end of the park sat the old Black school. School hadn't been held in it for years and it was getting run-down. Momma said some people tried to have it torn down once, but the mayor wouldn't let them do it. I liked that old school though, because it was the only one-room school I'd ever seen. More important, Daddy said he went to school there when he was a boy.

At the Dairy Queen, Alberta and I got double-dip chocolate-chip cones. Ethel couldn't decide what she wanted, so Momma bought her a vanilla cone. You know what that kid did? Dropped it! Momma just got her another one. Boy, that burned me up, but Alberta said I should tend to my business because Momma could do what she wanted with her own money.

That's when I decided I was going to do what I wanted with *my* own Sunday afternoon. I might practice some softball with Alberta or, if she didn't want to, I could bounce the ball off the coal shed in the backyard. Maybe I would go over to Gloria's and play. Then a honeybee zoomed over my head and I suddenly remembered my bees.

I kept honeybees in a jar filled with dandelion and clover blossoms. I figured the bees ought to produce honey in that jar. Well, they hadn't yet, but those things took time. After they became accustomed to their new home, I figured I could train them, the way people do with pigeons. I'd just caught a new batch of bees on Thursday but with Ethel coming and so much happening at home, I'd forgotten to go out and check on them. I bet they were starved.

Squirrels leaned on their tails in Mr. Everett's gravel driveway as we went by. I could see cardinals and blue jays dancing in the Aberdeens' front yard. What a great afternoon! I hoped I wouldn't have to fight with Momma to get away from Ethel.

What Miz Orange and Miz Wilkins said about Miz Mary popped in my head. When Momma got close enough, I asked her straight out. "When's Miz Mary coming back?"

"How many times have I said tonight?" she asked, flicking a drop of ice cream off her upper lip.

"I know, but Miz Wilkins told me what Miz Mary did to the Swensens, and Miz Orange said—"

"Margie, what you heard was gossip, and you know I don't approve of gossip," she replied. "The only bus that comes through here at night gets in around midnight, so I guess she'll have to be on that one."

Maybe Miz Mary would hitchhike back and surprise us. Maybe she'd be at our house right now, I thought, and crossed my fingers. But the porch was empty when we got there. I sighed. Well, I knew she ought to be on her way home. I went into our room, changed clothes, and hopped back out.

"I'm glad you put on old clothes, Margie," said Momma from the kitchen. "Would you help Ethel with her clothes, and then take her outside with you?"

I knew it! I knew she'd try to make me play with that kid. "I don't want to." I pulled my eyebrows down. "I can't have any fun with her around."

Momma said louder, "You and Ethel play, please."

I jangled the knob of the back-porch door. "How come I've gotta change her ole clothes and play with her?"

"Because you're closer to her," Alberta said wickedly.

I slapped my hands against my thighs and jiggled my legs, but I still ended up helping Ethel. I snatched at the buttons on her dress and hoped they would pop off. Momma knew I didn't like to play with little kids. Why did she keep picking on me?

"There!" I gave Ethel a shove. "You can take it off yourself."

Ethel lifted the dress up over her head, but the waist part stuck around her forehead. I just laughed. "Don't even know how to get it off," I told her. "I'll sure be glad when your momma comes. Here, girl. Now step out of this ole dress. You're a troublesome ole thing."

"I don't like you." Ethel squinched up her lips and made her fingers into claws.

"Hit me and I'll brain you! Now hang up that dress!"

My hands went to my hips. I knew the normal, evil Ethel had to show itself sometime, and there it was! "Don't nobody want to play with you, neither."

"Momma said I could play with you," Ethel sneered.

"Your momma's not here!"

Ethel pointed to the kitchen. "That momma in there said I could."

"She did not!"

"Did too!"

"Did not!"

"Margie, mind your manners."

I must have jumped ten feet in the air. Momma was standing in the door. She probably had seen everything. I tried to slink past her, but I could feel her eyes burning into my back. When we got outside Ethel jumped down the porch steps ahead of me, so I turned to see if Momma was around. She wasn't. Know what I did? Yanked one of those frizzy curls hard.

"Ow!"

But somebody else saw. From the kitchen window Alberta said, "Momma's gonna get you, girl."

Hearing Alberta's warning, Ethel got smart and hauled off and hit me in the back with her fist. I drew back my hand to smack her good.

"Don't you hit her, Margie," Alberta said.

"Well, she hit me!"

"You started it," Alberta said, "and she's only four years old."

Alberta had some nerve. She could talk like that because she didn't have to play with Ethel. I stalked around the house to get my bees with that brat tramping right behind me. As soon as I looked in the jar though I knew the bees had died. Their golden, velvet bodies lay there like fuzzy yellow buttons. "See!" I pushed the jar at Ethel. "Now you gotta catch me some more."

"I don't wanna get no bees." Ethel looked at me like I was crazy. "I wanna ride your bike."

"Well, you can't."

Ethel poked out her lips, doubled up her fists, and struck out at me. Then she ran back to the house, her hair flying behind her. I was glad she was gone, and I'd be even gladder when she was gone for good. Miz Mary might be coming back right now, I thought. She'd knock on our door and talk a little bit, then she and Ethel would leave and that would be the end of that. I spied a honeybee resting on a pink-and-white clover blossom. Emptying the jar, I quickly steadied my hand and went after it.

Just then Alberta hollered, "Momma said for you to take Ethel for a ride on your bike!"

I banged up to the back-porch steps. "I don't want that ole thing on my bike!" I threw my jar out into the yard.

Momma's voice came sharply. "Margie, I thought I asked you to do something. And Alberta, you help, too."

Alberta's shoulders dropped. We came out on the front porch and saw that Ethel was trying to get on my three-speed. "I get to ride your bike," she said.

"It's too big for you," I told her. Ethel tried to stand the bike up straight against the porch pillar, but it crashed to the ground, her with it. She let out a shriek.

"Girl!" I ran to my bike and lifted it while Alberta helped Ethel to her feet. The fender was bent and the seat was crooked. When Momma looked out the door, Alberta hurriedly brushed Ethel off. Momma went away.

Now was the time to fix Ethel. "Okay," I said. "I'll take you for a ride, but you gotta finish it yourself."

Alberta looked at me curiously. "Where you going?" she asked.

"To the hill." Around the corner was a steep driveway at an old, empty house. That was where I had learned to ride when I was seven. Alberta had sat me on my new bike at the top of the driveway and pushed me off to get me started. After the dust from the gravel had settled, I was at the bottom of the driveway with my knee split open and my elbows all skinned up and bleeding. When Daddy got home and heard about it, he tanned Alberta good.

"No, Ethel, you stay here," I heard Alberta say as I started to wheel my bike out of the yard. "She's just trying to get you hurt and get me in trouble."

Well, maybe that kid would have got hurt. I guess I didn't want to break up all her bones. I guess I just wanted her to go! So I put my bike up and Alberta and I went to our room.

Of course Ethel came, too. I pulled my basket of seashells from under my bed and held my favorite conch shell to my ear.

"What's that?" Ethel got down on the floor and nearly sat on top of me trying to see. Alberta, who was lying on her bed removing her nail polish, snickered.

"Get off me." I had to elbow Ethel back. "They're my shells." Ethel reached for the basket, but I pushed her away. "You better leave them alone," I said. "They don't belong to you. I bet you don't have anything like these."

"Do, too," she answered, staring at them. "I got a million million shells, all pretty, too."

"Margie, if you don't want her to play with them, you better put them up," Alberta said.

"I wanna play with them," Ethel said.

I carefully set my conch shell back in the basket and pushed it way under the bed. "Go play with your own shells, since you got so many."

Ethel turned to Alberta. "Put some polish on me, too," she demanded.

Well, you know who had to do it—*me!* Alberta didn't have any polish left, she said. But everybody could see my full bottle.

For the rest of the afternoon, it seemed like, I was smearing nail polish on that kid's fingers. I felt like I couldn't stand being around her another minute. What a boring Sunday! After dinner when Momma was in the kitchen, I snuck outside—alone—and ran over to visit Miz Moten.

She was working in her garden, dropping seeds into a furrow. "Can I help?" I asked. "What you planting this time?"

"Puttin' in some more greens, baby. You can take a little dirt and cover them seeds," she said. She pushed back the sleeves of her ole black sweater and rested for a minute. "Gettin' too old to do all this hoein'. Your daddy get off okay, did he?"

"Yeah. Ain't you hot in that sweater?"

"No, baby." When she grinned I could see the pink parts of her false teeth. She spit out some snuff. "You stay busy and your daddy be back before you know it."

"Hope Miz Mary is, too," I said.

Miz Moten looked at me. "Meaning your guest ain't gone yet and you dyin' for her to go. When she supposed to leave? I saw her come."

"Tonight, I guess."

"Well," Miz Moten said, and spit again. Momma didn't care for her habit of dipping snuff and spitting, but I thought it was funny. Miz Moten once gave me a little bit of snuff. I just sneezed. We were good friends.

When I finished helping Miz Moten with her planting, I told her good-bye and came back to our front porch. Alberta sat on the steps oiling her hair. "Your eyes are gonna fall out of your head," she said, "the way you keep gawking up and down the street looking for Miz Mary."

"You're gawking, too," I told her. Up the street I saw

Mr. Benjamin, another grown-up friend of mine, drive around a corner on his grass cutter. He must have been cutting the grass along the highway nearby. "You think Miz Mary might hitchhike back? Then she could get home before midnight."

"Just as long as she gets here."

So we sat together and watched for Miz Mary until it got dark. Alberta even helped me count lightning bugs and the chirps of crickets crooning from under the house.

"Wonder what Daddy's doing right now," I said, tired of counting.

"Probably driving that big ole truck, or sleeping."

"I hope he's all right." Sometimes I had nightmares about Daddy getting hurt. Momma never talked about Daddy getting hurt in an accident, but I know she thought about it. I did, lots of times, and that would make me cry. Momma listened to the late, late news on television every night, and when the television went off she'd turn on the radio in her room. Once about four o'clock in the morning I woke up and heard the San Antonio, Texas, news. Another time I heard a talk show from St. Louis. Momma always tried to tune in a radio station near wherever she thought Daddy was.

"You think he's ate supper yet?"

"Now you *know* Daddy's gonna eat," Alberta reminded me.

Daddy could eat a whole two-layer cake and a plate of fried chicken and three helpings of mashed potatoes at one meal and still come back looking for a snack.

It wouldn't be so bad if Daddy would call home, but he hardly ever did. Daddy said we would worry too much if we knew exactly where he was. Once he'd been driving somewhere in Mississippi when he ran into a flood. He'd had to climb out of the truck and onto the roof when water came surging across the yards and through the streets. Daddy made it sound funny when he told us, but Momma hadn't laughed.

The June summer night was so pretty I forgot my troubles and pretended that the sparkles in the damp evening grass were lanterns carried by snails and slugs. But just then Ethel had to come clattering out on the front porch. "Momma said I can sleep in your bed."

"Whose momma?"

Ethel put her hand on her hip. "The momma in the house."

"That's *my* momma." I stood up and put *both* hands on my hips to show her I wasn't going to take any more of that stuff. She finally backed off and went inside.

"Miz Mary's coming back tonight, isn't she, Alberta? Momma said she was."

Alberta looked back at me, not smiling or anything. "Well, that's what Momma said."

Daddy always told me that if you thought hard enough about something you want to come true, then it probably would. So I thought real hard about Miz Mary coming and about Daddy coming home. I thought so hard I fell asleep and Alberta had to wake me up.

"You better go on to bed, girl," she said, "else I'm gonna let you fall off the steps."

I yawned, stood up, and went to bed, careful to stay away from Ethel. She seemed to be sound asleep. I bet she'd never slept in a bed as nice as mine. And as far as I was concerned, tonight would be the last time, too.

5

But when I woke up Monday morning Ethel was still there, and she had taken all the covers, too. Miz Mary hadn't come back? But Momma had said she was going to, and Momma wouldn't lie to us! Then I discovered that Ethel had peed up the bed again.

"You dummy, you pee pot!" I jumped up from my side and swooped down on her. Ethel woke up quick, grabbed one of my braids, and tried to yank it out of my head. My fingers raked at her hands, and my knees jabbed in her stomach. She pulled so hard, though, my head felt like Momma had burned me with the pressing comb!

"Get out of here, get out!" I punched at every part of her. Nasty thing peeing in my bed when she was supposed to be gone!

Smack! Smack! Smack! "I told you!" Momma was shouting and whacking me hard on my behind. "I told you not to fight. Now you get back in that bed and you stay there!"

"Momma, Momma, I didn't do it! She peed in my— Momma, why's she still here?" I fell back on that stinky bed and bawled as Momma guided Ethel out of the room.

Boy, I cried and kicked and screamed and bounced on my bed and cried some more. To be spanked was bad enough, but to be spanked unfairly was the worst. Alberta crept in like she was scared. I could feel her standing by me, so I hollered even louder. "Momma's always blaming me! She's always taking up for that ole trashy half-white thing!"

Daddy wouldn't have let Momma spank me. He'd have heard my side first. Like that time Momma was going to chew me out because I broke one of those ole precious plates Grandmother Ralston gave us. I hadn't meant to. Daddy had told Momma that if she was so worried about the plates she should wash them herself.

I cried myself to sleep, and didn't wake up again until the noon whistle blew at the paint factory. After what

Momma had done I didn't feel like ever moving again, but I was too hungry to stay in bed. I went to the kitchen and made myself a peanut butter, mayonnaise, and tomato sandwich. The house was quiet. Maybe that meant Miz Mary had come back and taken Ethel. Or maybe Momma had felt ashamed of spanking her own kid and sent Ethel off to the Children's Home.

A while later Momma came into the kitchen alone and asked if I wanted something to drink. I just nodded and bit into my sandwich. She poured me a glass of milk and sat down at the table. "You think I'm a mean mother, hmmm?" she asked.

I shook my head, and then I nodded yes. Momma went on, "Well, honey, I hate to spank my girls, but you know how I feel about fighting. I didn't spank you when you and Alberta fought yesterday, but when you got into it with Ethel, I couldn't let it go by. Sometimes a swat or two can get across a message when words can't. Do you think you understand?"

I got the message—I got a spanking, but Ethel and Alberta didn't. "You're not supposed to fight Alberta because she's older and stronger," Momma said, "and more importantly, because she's your sister. You're not supposed to fight Ethel because Ethel's still a little girl. She's also a guest in our house and everyone has to help her."

"But Ethel always starts it," I finally told her. "If she wasn't here I wouldn't have to fight."

"You're not used to having her around." Momma

kept talking like she hadn't even heard me. "But she's here and you must understand that. You need to learn to share. If something doesn't go your way, you just have to learn to deal with it like a lady, like Grandmother Ralston and I do. Don't you want to do like I do?"

I couldn't say no to that. "But Ethel—"

"We have to teach Ethel how to behave like a lady, too, and fighting and being mean to her won't do it."

"But I was trying to teach her not to pee in my bed."

"What?"

"Not to wet my bed, I mean." I wanted to ask if ladies peed in the bed. I wanted to ask if it was fair that I had to get spanked while Ethel and Alberta didn't. I kept quiet, though, because Momma wasn't paying any attention to what I said.

"You're the younger of my girls, so that makes you the baby. But when your birthday comes you'll be ten, and that's mighty old for a baby. You can help Ethel not be a baby either."

Ethel again! I cupped my face in my hands. "But Momma, why is she still here?"

"Miz Mary called late last night and said that something came up," she said slowly. "She said she won't be able to get back until next Monday."

"But Momma, that's a whole week from now!" The tears I'd been holding back began to fall at last.

"It won't be forever, Margie."

"Not even Grandmother Ralston or Uncle Jake ever

stays with us for a whole week. How come *she's* got to be here all that time?" I cried.

I had to wait a long time before Momma answered. "If we hadn't taken her in, no one else would have because everybody says she's bad. She would have been put in the Children's Home, and that wouldn't have been good for her."

"You don't leave me and Alberta with other people. How come Miz Mary couldn't take Ethel with her?"

"Because"—and Momma sighed—"because she just couldn't! Try to understand, honey. Ethel's just a little girl who needs a nice home where people care about her until her mother returns."

"I don't care about her. How come you have to?" I ran the back of my hand over my eyes.

Momma came over to me and gently wiped my cheek with her fingers. "I care because I wouldn't want to see you or Alberta just out in the street with nobody to look after you. I don't want to see any child just dumped like that." She pecked me on my forehead and then she took up a strainer full of green beans and left the kitchen.

That kiss made me feel a little better. I ate some more of my sandwich. What if Momma did leave, and Alberta and Daddy weren't around? Wow, that was a scary thought. But I knew Momma wouldn't ever be gone. Momma wasn't Miz Mary, taking off, leaving her kids around.

I looked out the window. The leaves of Momma's geranium on the sill were hanging limp like sheets on the clothesline. She had forgot to water it, I bet, and that wasn't like her. I studied that plant. Maybe if I watered it Momma would see that I was thinking about her. So I did.

On the back porch Momma and Ethel were breaking string beans. "Ethel's a good bean breaker," Momma said to me. "She can go even faster than I can."

"Where's Alberta?" I asked. A small, cool breeze was dancing in through the screen and Momma's radio was playing.

"She went over to Miz Orange's to wash her dishes, so I thought we'd do these beans for her."

I peered at the pile of beans in Ethel's bowl. "She's throwing away a lot of the good part," I said.

"Then why don't you show her how to do it right?"

To do a green bean, you have to pinch off the heads and tails with your forefinger and thumb nails. Then you snap the bean apart. If they're long beans you can snap them two or three times. And if they're stringy, you have to unzip the threads.

So I came outside and tried to show Ethel. I knew she wouldn't do it right. And she didn't. She poked out her lips and knocked her bowl to the floor. "Aw, girl. See, Momma?" I frowned up at Momma.

"Thank you, Ethel." Momma just put a smile on her face. "You've helped us enough."

Momma wouldn't ever get after Ethel. I sighed. Well, I still didn't like her, and I didn't plan to like her for a whole week.

"I watered your geranium," I told Momma.

"Why, thank you, Margie." She smiled, and that made me feel better.

"Can we have some tapioca pudding for supper?"

"Maybe."

Ethel watched me and Momma break beans. I ignored her. Finally she kicked at a bean on the floor, and after fiddling around, slowly picked it up and looked at it. She picked up another bean. Looked at it. She picked them all up. One of her forefingers played around with a bean and do you know what happened? She pinched off both ends neat and broke the bean in half!

"That's the way!" Momma said, beaming like she'd just seen Daddy pull the car into the driveway.

So we sat and broke beans and then Momma let me wash them in the sink. She poured them in the kettle, added onions and garlic and a beef bone, shook in some pepper, and began to peel potatoes. I stayed at the kitchen table and watched hard because I wanted to learn how to cook. I was also trying to avoid having to play with Ethel. Did Alberta know she'd be staying for a whole week? That kid would tear my life into a million rotten pieces by the end of it.

The screen door slammed and Alberta walked in. Her hair was blown all over her head and her fingers looked red and wrinkled.

"How did it go with Miz Orange?" Momma asked.

"Same dishes, same hard work," said Alberta. She came to stand by Momma, who was carving on a slab of wood at the kitchen table while dinner cooked. Momma used to try to do needlepoint, but she said that was one part of being a lady that she couldn't stand. She took up woodcarving instead.

"She gave me three dollars this time," Alberta said as she peered at the carving. "What're you making now?"

"A platter with flowers with an outline of Africa in the middle." She frowned. "But I can't carve out the bulge of Africa the way I want."

I was dying to tell Alberta about Ethel staying for a whole week, but I couldn't get in a word. "Momma," asked Alberta, "when's Daddy supposed to come home?"

"Oh, he's on a long haul. I don't expect him to get back for two or three weeks."

"Daddy ought to call more often," said Alberta. "Anything could happen at home."

Momma gave her a sharp look, but she didn't say anything.

Alberta got to watching Momma like she knew a secret. "What would he say if he knew Ethel was here?"

"Why do you ask me that?"

"I just wondered." Alberta wandered off to our room, and I ran after her.

"Momma said Ethel's gonna stay for a whole week!" I closed the door. I didn't see Ethel, but maybe she was taking a nap in Momma's room.

"I know," Alberta replied. "Momma told me while you were in here throwing your legs around and bawling this morning. And I bet Daddy didn't know Ethel came and I bet he doesn't know she's gonna be here for a while." Alberta stretched out on her bed, studying her wrinkled fingers. "He'd be mad, too, if he came home suddenly and found her here."

"He'd say Ethel couldn't stay," I added. "If Daddy came home and Ethel was still here, he wouldn't let her stay. Where would she go?"

"Someplace else, that's for sure." She sat up. "Miz Orange talked about Ethel for days! You know what she said? She said Ethel had Black blood in her. Everybody knows that, but doesn't it sound funny?"

"But Miz Mary's not Black."

"That means, dummy, that her ole man's Black. That would make Ethel part Black," Alberta informed me. I asked her what else Miz Orange said. "She said Momma was acting like a white folks' nigger by having trash up in her house."

White folks' nigger? Some people I'd heard had called Momma stuck up because she always tried to do everything correct and ladylike. "Momma's not a white folks' nigger!" I got hot.

"You know what I did? Miz Orange had this big stack of pots and pans and skillets piled up on the table. Girl, I bumped into that table and knocked everything on the floor."

I giggled. Served that ole gossip right, calling Momma names. "But what'll Momma do to you when she finds out about it?" I asked. "Miz Orange'll tell."

"Momma won't do nothin' 'cause Miz Orange won't tell. She knows that if she does, I'll tell Momma what Miz Orange called her. And you keep your mouth shut, too, hear?" She walked over to the mirror and started to rearrange her hair. "I sure didn't like riding my bike home after all that work. I wish we had a car."

"We got a car."

"Yeah, but what good does it do us when Daddy always leaves it at work in Gillespie? I mean a car right here with us." She got to sighing and frowning. "I'm tired of walking everywhere. And I can't be riding my bike when I'm dressed up. I hate tramping up and down the street all the time, 'cause I got to dodge all that nasty stuff the tractors leave all over the place."

I liked tractors, and pickup trucks, too. Sometimes they pulled loads of corncobs, and corn dust would fly around. You could always tell when they carried pigs. Whew! "Ain't nothing wrong with tractors," I said.

"You like everything, 'cause you don't know nothing. Wait until you get older."

"But Alberta, what good would a car do us at home anyway? Momma can't drive."

"Billy Ray's mother knows how to drive," she fussed. "Momma's got ladylike on the brain. She told me once it wasn't ladylike to drive. That's stupid! I think she's just too scared to learn."

There went Alberta. "You've been around Miz Orange too long, girl, talking about Momma like that. Momma's not scared."

"Well, Momma's always talking about being a lady and how things were way down south when she was little and how Grandmother Ralston taught her all the proper things to do. Nobody pays any attention to that ole stuff anymore."

I kept quiet. It seemed to me that Alberta was doing a lot of talking about Momma, and what she was saying didn't sound nice. I was still a little mad at Momma myself, though. So I decided to just lay back and read a book and forget about Alberta and Momma and Ethel and figure out how Sherlock Holmes would solve his next murder.

6

Tuesday morning dragged in dark and rainy. That put Momma in a cleaning mood, so I had to clean up my side of our room. It was a mess and you know why. When I swept out something sparkly near the foot of my bed, I thought it was a dime until I looked closer.

"If you keep breaking up your shells you won't have any left," I told Alberta.

"Must be yours." Alberta didn't look up from her

book. "I don't play and kiss on my shells like you do. I only broke one, and that was a long time ago."

"I only broke one, too."

I got down and peered under my bed. Mixed in with the dustballs were broken snail shells, two arms off my starfish, and the head of my sea horse. The basket was squished up against the mattress. "My shells!" I pulled at the basket. "They're all broke up!"

Alberta squatted beside me and looked. "Oh, wow, Margie, that's terrible. Maybe you can glue some back together."

I had been so proud of my shells. I'd taken the first ones to school right after Daddy gave them to me. My teacher, Miz Worsum, had shown them to the class and I'd stood at the front of the room and talked all about them. Tears poured down my face and dripped into the basket. This ole dead day was the worst I'd ever known.

And I knew who'd been sneaking around under my bed. "I hate that Ethel! Hate her! But when I tell Momma she won't do a thing!"

"How do you know Ethel did it?"

"'Cause I didn't. Did you?"

"You know I wouldn't do a thing like that," said Alberta. "I'll go get Momma."

Something horrible had happened every day since Ethel came. Momma just yesterday had done all that talking about how I was supposed to teach Ethel to behave. How could I teach somebody so bad, so mean?

Momma came rushing in. She bent down and put

her arms around me. "Oh, what a shame," she said.

I barely heard her. My eyes were blurred with tears. My head hurt. My throat was thick and my nose was runny. There wasn't any use in saying a single word.

"Did your basket fall off the bed?" she asked. I shook my head. "Do you think you might have hit it when you swept under your bed?"

"No, Momma," Alberta said for me, "because she never sweeps under the bed."

Momma began, "Well, maybe you—"

"Ethel did it!" I finally screamed. Momma knew that! She knew it, but she had to keep asking all those stupid questions.

"Ethel?" Momma went to the door. "Ethel, come in here. Were you playing with Margie's shells? Did you break them?"

Ethel slouched into our room and stood by the door, shaking her head. Momma took her by the hand and walked her over to me. "Ethel, did you break Margie's shells?" she asked in a real soft, sweet voice. Ethel shook her head. She had her lips drawn down toward her chin like she was trying to cry.

Momma kept saying she didn't know how it could have happened, using her ole teacher talk. "Alberta didn't do it, Margie didn't do it, and I didn't do it. Who did it, Ethel? Won't you say something, honey?"

"Momma, Ethel's not going to talk," Alberta finally said. "She didn't even say she was sorry for tearing up Miz Silk's store."

"Thank you, Alberta, but we're not discussing Miz Silk's store," Momma said icily. Then she started back on Ethel with her sweet talk.

Alberta looked at Momma like she was disgusted. "Margie, you can have some of my shells," she said.

That really made me feel bad. I just shook my head. My seashells were gone. Momma couldn't bring them back to normal like when she washed my smelly sheets and pajamas. And all she had to say to me was that she was sorry and that she didn't know how it happened?

"Couldn't nobody have done it but *her!*" I jumped up and threw my basket to the floor. "I hate her!"

I ran out of the house down to the peach tree and cried against its bark. If Daddy were here he would make things all right. He would tell me that he knew people hadn't treated me fair. He'd come back and make the right decisions and not treat me like I was just an ole dirty rag. The rain soaked my clothes and braids, but I didn't go back inside. Why should I, when Momma didn't care about me, anyway?

The rain slowed down to a drizzle, but I stayed under the peach tree and let its leaves hang down around me. After a while I saw Miz Moten come out her back door with a bag. She had on her black galoshes and her plastic rain hat. She clanged open her garbage can and plopped the bag in. Then she looked across the yard at me.

"Honey, you better get on in the house! You catch pneumonia!" But when I stayed put, she clumped over.

"Chile," she said kindly, "what you doin' out here in this rain?" When I told her about Ethel breaking up my shells and peeing in my bed, and nobody caring, she said, "Humph, humph, humph. That gal's a pistol, ain't she? No need you gettin' wet over her, though. Come on home with me and drink this hot Dr Pepper I'ma fix for ya."

Miz Moten had a little bitty house. We went into the front room, where she kept her wood cookstove, her cot, her dresser, and her boxes and trunks of clothes. "Can I use your bathroom?" I asked.

"Go head, baby," she said, "and take that towel in there, dry your hair."

Miz Moten called her bathroom her closet. It had a toilet, a basin, and a little bathtub with clawed feet. Her outhouse still sat in the backyard and that bothered Momma all to death. But Miz Moten wouldn't tear it down. She said she was afraid her closet would get stopped up, and then she wouldn't have a pot to pee in.

When I came out Miz Moten had the Dr Pepper bubbling on the stove. She always had something around good for me to drink. One time she even gave me a little taste of elderberry wine. She handed me some hot Dr Pepper in a big tin cup. I sat real close to her cookstove because I'd gotten cold.

"Yeah, that gal's a pistol," she repeated. She still had on her boots and her scarf.

"She sure is. Momma just loves her, though."

"Your momma love everybody. Don't be too hard on your momma, baby. She just doin' what she thinks is right." She slurped on her own drink. "Shame about them pretty shells. I sure did like to see them when you carried them over. Well, look like you not the baby anymore."

"I'm not a baby."

"You sure ain't, not with Ethel there." Miz Moten drank up her Dr Pepper. "You the middle sister now, ain't ya?"

"Ethel ain't my sister!" I glared at Miz Moten like she was nuts.

"Now you ain't got to roll them big eyes at *me*." She clicked her false teeth, but she didn't do it to make fun. "I'm sayin' you in the middle and they ain't lettin' you get the due you used to havin' 'cause they's somebody younger around right now." She reached for her little red can of snuff, took out a pinch, and tucked it between her lower false teeth and lip.

She didn't mind me watching her do that. She said she was an old southern woman and dipping was what old southern women did. I wondered if Grandmother Ralston dipped.

"Gonna be a whole lot of things Ethel's gonna do that you won't like, baby. But it won't be up to you to turn things around. You got enough to do just makin' sure you grow up pretty and smart. Can't be gettin' your behind up on your shoulders worrying over that gal. Too much trouble tryin' to get it back down."

"Miz Mary's coming back." I didn't know why I had to tell her that, but I didn't want to hear Miz Moten talk the same way as Miz Orange and Miz Wilkins. All her talk about me being in the middle made it seem like Ethel had moved in for good.

"You warm now, baby?" she asked. "How that Dr Pepper taste?"

"It was good. Thanks, Miz Moten. I better go back." I really didn't want to, though.

"You welcome anytime." She went to the back door with me and held it open. "You stay out of that rain."

I ran back and sat on the damp front porch, but I hadn't been there more than five minutes before Ethel came out. She stood there with her stupid finger in her mouth. "Leave me alone," I said. The way I had been feeling came rushing up inside me again. "Ole trashy thing. You sure are a humdinger and an ole pee pot."

Ethel moved her toes in her ole sandals, staring so hard at me that I wished she'd look someplace else. Finally she whispered, "Ain't trashy and ain't no humdinger."

"You are, too. And you're a smelly, ole ugly dummy and a fart," I spat as nasty as I could. "Stinky thing! Why'd you break up my stuff?"

When she shook her head, I got really hot. "You did, too, and I know you did. You can talk now, hunh. You did it! Say it! And Momma didn't even get after you!" I balled up my fists. "My shells are smashed! They weren't yours!"

"I was just playin' with 'em," she said and got to whimpering like she had when her ole momma first threw her off on us. "You got pretty shells. I was just playin' with 'em and then Alberta came home and I was puttin' 'em back and I dropped the basket off the bed and they kept breakin' up—"

" 'Cause you broke 'em up!" I frowned so hard at her my face hurt. "You can't be going around messing with other people's things. You said you had a million shells. You're a liar! How'd you like me breaking up your shells? But you ain't got any, do you?"

"No," she said, snotting and crying.

"You want me to break up your stuff?"

"Ain't got no stuff." She rubbed her fists in her eyes.

"You got toys!"

"Ain't got no toys."

"Not a doll or a car or a water pistol or building blocks? Not a yo-yo or a jumping rope or even a bunch of jacks?"

"Ain't got no doll, no yo-yo." She was bawling now.

I didn't believe her. Everybody had toys. "Well, what do you play with?"

"Gotta lotta bottles Momma got empty, bottle caps, got some rocks. But I ain't got no stuff."

"I'm gonna ask Momma and see." I marched straight into the house and found Momma sitting in the rocking chair in the living room. "Ethel said she broke my seashells," I told her.

"Well, I'm glad that she admitted it to you. Margie,

I'm really sorry that she broke them, I really am."

I wasn't sure she was, because she didn't look too sorry. "If I broke Alberta's stuff you'd spank me," I said.

"Maybe, maybe not. Ethel's been hit too much as it is," she said. Then she stopped and said real fast, "I mean, you have to be kind to her to get a message across. I'm sure she knows now that it was wrong for her to get into your shells without asking you first. And I talked to her."

"Ethel said she plays with bottles and rocks and junk," I said, looking Momma in the eye, "and that she doesn't have any toys, but I don't believe it."

Momma began to rock in that chair. "Bottles and junk, hunh? Isn't that a shame." She shook her head. "If that was all you had, I bet you'd want to play with somebody's pretty seashells and ride their bike and get polish on your fingernails, too. No, I'm sure she doesn't have any toys."

No toys? Not a single toy at all? Miz Mary must be awful mean, I thought. I went slowly back into our room and looked at my broken-up basket.

Alberta was still there, reading. "Are you all right?" she asked.

"Yeah. You know, Momma said I should understand that Ethel got into my shells because she doesn't have anything to play with." I still wasn't sure I believed it. "Ethel says she plays with bottles and stuff."

"Well, if that's all she has, then she sure doesn't have

any toys." Alberta chewed on her lip, then she went to the dresser and unlocked her little jewelry box. On the first shelf was a small shell that Alberta had once said looked like a bronze gem. She lifted it out and told me to give it to Ethel.

"She's just gonna break it up," I told her.

"Momma says if you have something, it's better to share it with somebody else, especially if you got a little extra." She lay back on her bed.

"You're crazy."

"You're selfish," she answered. "Maybe you'll under-stand when you get older."

I picked through my basket and found an unbroken coquina shell. Looked over at Alberta, but she had her head back in her book. When I got back to the front porch, Ethel was still there. "Here," I said.

She put out her hand and blinked when she saw Alberta's shell. "Thank you." Her face was one big smile and her nose was running.

"It's from Alberta," I explained. That was the first time I saw Ethel smile not because she'd done something terrible. "And you can borrow this one of mine while you're here," I added.

"Oh, Margie!" Her fingers grabbed at the shell so fast I thought she was gonna snatch off my hand, too. "Oh, thank you! I'm gonna show Momma!" She darted into the house.

There she went again with that "Momma" stuff. My mind buzzed. I wondered if I was crazy too. Why did I give her one of my shells after she'd broken almost all of them up?

While I tried to figure it out, Momma came onto the porch, smiling. "What a beautiful thing you did, Margie, to give your shell to Ethel. And if Daddy were here, he'd be very proud of you."

"He would?"

"He sure would." She tweaked one of my braids. "Now, I don't mean for you to give away everything you have, but what you did was a sign of maturity. Understanding. Rightness. I know it was a hard thing to do."

Right then I thought about what it would be like not having any toys. I had always thought everybody had toys. I guess that's why I decided to share with Ethel. And then I wondered if Momma realized my shell was just on loan.

7

Wednesday night was our softball game and it gave me something else to worry about. Would Momma want to take Ethel along? I knew I shouldn't even have bothered to worry, though, because when it was time to go I saw Ethel all dressed and ready. I sighed. Oh, well. I should have known.

"Who's going to win?" asked Momma from the bathroom.

"Nubia Missionary All Stars, of course," Alberta answered, punching her fist into her glove. She played first base and was the best player on the team.

"You're scared, Alberta. I bet you're gonna get run over by some player again," I told her. "You're gonna drop all the balls, and we won't get anybody out."

"You better shut up," she said. "Ethel told me you only loaned that shell to her. Does Momma know that?"

I shut up.

The Liberty Baptist Ladybugs were already on the field showing off their white T-shirts and red shorts when we got there. The All Stars came out in our white shirts and blue shorts and practiced, too, but at a safe distance. I was so nervous I had to line up our three bats over and over. Then I wanted to make sure everybody had their gloves, like I was supposed to.

"Would you go someplace?" Alberta snapped from first base. "This is pregame warm-up. Only official players supposed to be out on the field."

"Oh, Alberta," I said as I got off the field. Where did she get that pregame warm-up stuff? The All Stars just threw balls.

The big boys drove their ole fine Trans Ams and ole raggedy Mustangs on the grass at the far side of the field. Then they walked around laughing and talking loud. I saw Debbie Marshall run to the water faucet near our dugout and nearly drown herself getting a drink. Momma wouldn't let me drink by sticking my head under the faucet because she said it wasn't lady-like. But to me it looked like fun.

The green bleachers filled up quickly, but I could still see Ethel with Momma. I bet the Ladybugs could see Ethel, too. The Ladybugs came from Glenburg, which was fifteen miles away, but they probably knew who she was. Everybody in the whole county probably knew about Ethel and Miz Mary. Miz Orange stepped up the bleachers and set her fat self down by Momma.

"How're you doing, Margie?" asked Miz Jackson, our coach. Coach had a barrel stomach and ham-shaped hips and little bitty legs and a soft, smiling face. She looked like a grandmother, but she didn't have any kids. Coach always wore her husband's railroad cap to the game for good luck. But when she got mad, the hat came off and everybody would holler, "Look out!"

Missy Walker walked past a Ladybug outfielder near the fence. "Where's your friend Chester?" Missy said. "I don't see him anywhere." The Ladybug just smacked on her chewing gum. "Bet Chester's still out in the corn-field," Missy said, grinning. "You know you can't get that hoe from them country boys until ten o'clock."

"Is that ole ugly, gold-toothed thing talkin' to me?" the Ladybug asked another girl.

Missy slunk off the field.

When the game started, Gloria sat down on the bench beside me. I was glad to see her. Gloria was also bat girl. "You think they're gonna kill us again?" she asked.

"Yeah. How come you weren't at church? I got in trouble with Miz Hamlin."

"I had a cold. What you been doing?"

"Nothin'. I stayed outside almost all night last Sunday," I said.

Gloria put her finger by the cleft in her chin. "Waitin' for Miz Mary, hunh. You like having Ethel at your house?"

"How'd you know?"

"Missy told Sarah and Sarah told me, but I'da found out anyway 'cause everybody knows."

"What's everybody sayin'?"

"I don't know," she said at first, but she must have seen my face screw up. "Well, just stuff like they bet you and Alberta were goin' crazy and they bet your momma had to use ten tons of soap to clean her up. How you like havin' her around?"

Well, I sure couldn't tell Gloria about Ethel breaking up my shells or spitting on the carpet or making me get a spanking, because she'd tell everybody else. So I cleared my throat and said, "I don't know."

"You don't know?" Gloria laughed. "I sure wouldn't want a snot-nosed stinky thing like that around me."

"She's not stinky anymore. Momma keeps her clean. You know what, Gloria? That girl doesn't even have toys. She says she just plays with bottles and rocks."

"Yeah, them beer bottles from her momma, and rocks she throws at everybody." Gloria slowed down when she saw me start to get mad. "But I guess she likes it at your house, hunh?"

I didn't want to talk about Ethel anymore. "Look! Bases are loaded!" I yelled. "You see that big ole girl with the ponytail, the girl up to bat? Last time she hit a home run with bases loaded because everybody was so busy gawking and gossiping they let the ball go over their heads."

Crack! Home run. Four to nothing.

"We better go wake up our outfield," Gloria said, groaning. We ran to the sidelines, yelling. "Get 'em out! Get 'em out!"

"Bring 'em in!" the Ladybugs yelled right back from their dugout.

So we had a shouting match, with everybody on our team hollering to get the players out and the Ladybugs hollering to bring them in to score.

Our cheering helped, I think. The Ladybugs only made three more runs before we finally got them out. Seven to nothing. The All Stars came up to bat, then they struck out three in a row and went right back out on the field.

I was getting so discouraged that I ran over to the bleachers and crept under them until I came up close to Momma. "They're tough again, aren't they?" she said when she saw me. "You girls will have to get on the stick."

Ethel squinched up her shoulders. "Momma said get on the stick." Miz Orange got to laughing so hard she had a coughing fit. Ethel grinned like she thought she said something smart. I couldn't stand it. I ducked back down under the bleachers and ran out again to the dug-out.

Two innings went by. We had held the Ladybugs to seven runs and the Ladybugs had held us to none. Alberta strolled around the dugout, rubbing her legs. To get extra energy she pulled a sugar cube from her pocket and sucked on it.

"Ethel said for you to get on the stick," I told her. "And Coach is gonna make you practice all day tomorrow if we lose. I bet I could score if I was old enough to play."

Alberta waved away my words as she went over to home plate. It was her turn at bat. Ball one. We all cheered. Strike one, strike two, foul ball.

"C'mon, Alberta," screamed Georgia.

Then from out of the bleachers floated Ethel's voice: "Get on the stick!"

Suddenly Alberta swung hard. The softball fell out in the field. Alberta flew around first, second, then headed for third, but an outfielder grabbed up the ball and hurled it like a bullet to third. When Alberta went back toward second, so did the ball.

"Oh, Alberta!" Sandy picked up her pitcher's mitt. I just peeked through my fingers.

When Alberta again headed back toward third, the second baseman threw the ball after her. It soared over the third baseman's head. Safe at third, Alberta then streaked for home with the Ladybug catcher straddling home plate, waiting. She dived forward and slid on her stomach between the catcher's fat legs.

"Safe!" yelled the umpire.

We all ran to Alberta, clapped her on her back, and helped brush off the dust on her shorts and shirt. I was so proud! But Missy had to goggle-eye her and hiss, "Alberta got on Ethel's stick, no lie."

"Sure did, didn't she?" Coach said. "Maybe I ought to start yelling it, too, and get the rest of you gals going. Good job, Alberta. Now you gals get off the field, quick!"

The Ladybugs finally trounced us, fourteen to one, but I didn't really care. If it hadn't been for my sister we wouldn't have even had one run. That was why she was still the best player. We went out and shook hands with the Ladybugs after the game to show we were good sports. Then I grabbed Alberta's glove from Gloria and wiggled it at Momma.

Alberta and I were hanging around the dugout with the All Stars, talking about what we needed to work on, when Missy suddenly began to shout. "Lookit, a fight! Alberta's momma's in a fight!"

We looked over at the bleachers to see Momma and Miz Lucy Good standing toe to toe and yelling at each other. As people bunched around them, Alberta and I hurried over. Our momma in a fight?

"Who you callin' nosy, Sister Prissy?" screamed Miz Good. "You skinny, dried-up—"

"When I want you to know what's going on at one seventeen Jamison, I'll bring in another bed and invite you over!" Momma answered angrily.

"Don't think there'd be room!" Miz Good shot back.

"Ain't all of us so crazy about white trash up in our faces the way you are. You'd never got that teaching job if you hadn't been licking up on—"

"You don't know a thing about it!" Momma's voice went high. "I am a fully certified, qualified—"

"You can just shut up!"

"—teacher and you're just jealous—"

"Jealous of what?" Miz Good reared back, waggled her head, and sneered, "Of some half-breed daughter of a white-trash whore?"

Everybody went "oh!" My mouth fell open. We tried to push in close, but the grown folks wouldn't let us.

Miz Orange threw up her big fat arms and pushed Momma and Miz Good apart. "Now we can't have no talk like that with all these children around! And you are jealous, Lucy, 'cause Luvenia's a teacher and you still cleanin' and waxin' floors!"

"And you! You fat cow! Don't you defend her!" Miz Good jumped up and down like she was going to take on Momma and Miz Orange, too. "White folks' niggers, both of you!"

Momma backed away. "I won't listen to this garbage! I won't listen to it!" She spun out of the crowd with Ethel and strode off. Before I knew it, she'd left the softball park and was burning up the street.

Alberta caught up with her, but I stayed back a little. Nobody had told *me* Miz Mary was a whore. Everybody seemed to know something but me!

Well, I did know a little bit about Miz Good. She and

Momma never had hit it off. They wouldn't even speak in church. Once I heard Momma and Miz Orange talking about it. Miz Good was supposed to be jealous because when they integrated the schools here Miz Good had been a maid in the school. She didn't like it one bit when Momma got a teaching job right after she graduated from college in Atlanta, Georgia. Momma was the only Black teacher in town and everybody else mostly liked her. But Miz Good wouldn't clean up her homeroom. Miz Good told somebody, who told Miz Orange, who of course told Momma, that she would never clean up after a colored person, especially one who wasn't a relative. So Momma always cleaned her own room, and it was the cleanest room in the whole high school.

I kept getting closer to Momma and Alberta, and I heard Momma say, "I'd rather not discuss it."

I finally got caught up with them and was about to ask Momma what she thought of the game when Momma said to Alberta, "I was afraid you'd get called out. You didn't hurt yourself sliding in, did you?"

"No, but I had to slide, you know," Alberta said. "I didn't want to run into that brick wall blocking the plate."

Momma looked at me. "Well, Margie, you picked up a few more bats this time, didn't you?"

"Yeah." Momma always praised me about those bats. Just let her wait until I turned ten and actually played! "We got to practice tomorrow."

A small hot hand grabbed at mine. Ethel. She must have come unhooked from Momma. I threw Alberta's glove high, caught it, and skipped away. It was nighttime behind us now and twilight in front. Between the branches of the trees I could see the violet sky.

The mosquitoes followed the twilight. Ethel got to slapping and fussing, but nobody paid her any attention. "Momma," said Alberta, "when are you going to learn to drive?"

"Probably never. I can get where I want by walking or taking the taxi. Besides, this isn't a big place like Kansas City. Are you too weak or too grown to walk?"

"I'm just tired of riding my bike or walking everywhere. Walking is so country."

Momma put a little fire in her voice. It reminded me of how she had sounded during the fight. "Well, dear, you're living in a country town. Why, we don't have a TV station, the radio plays country music, the fire station and the paint factory tell people when it's time for lunch and dinner, and we've got farmers still coming to town spitting snuff and tobacco all over. And certain people still have outhouses."

Momma cleared her throat. "Did I see that boy there at the game?"

"What boy?" Alberta asked.

Uh-oh, here it comes again, I thought.

"That Billy Ray Morgan. Was he out there with those punks at the end of the field?"

I saw Alberta stiffen. "I don't know any punks. But all the guys go stand by the cars, Momma. I didn't see him, but if he was out there he wasn't doing anything wrong."

"All that drinking they do back there," Momma fussed. "All that cussing and carrying on."

"That doesn't mean Billy Ray does it."

"Well, you can tell about a boy from the company he keeps, and if he hangs around with punks he's going to be a punk. You just make sure you stay away from him." Momma's voice began to get that high sound to it again.

"There's nothing wrong with him," Alberta shot back.

"He better keep away from you, that's for sure," Momma snapped.

Alberta tightened her hands into fists. If it had been lighter outside I knew I would have seen Momma's and Alberta's cheeks turn red. "Momma, you just don't like him because his family is on welfare!"

She stamped down the street, but Momma walked faster and caught her by the arm. "I'm not going to allow my children to associate with people who don't want to uplift themselves and their race and lead proper, productive lives!"

Alberta wheeled around. "Well, what do you call Miz Mary and Ethel? Everybody knows that Ethel's daddy is Black and that Miz Mary is a whore!"

Momma drew back her hand like she was about to hit

Alberta. But just as her hand was about to flash out, Ethel hollered.

"Momma!" she cried. "We can't fight! You said not to fight!"

Momma looked down at Ethel. Then she lowered her hand and walked slowly on toward our house.

Boy, Momma had really scared me. I never knew she would want to slap us. It seemed like everybody had been fighting since Ethel came.

Then I got to thinking about that kid. She'd finally remembered something that Momma had tried to teach her. Was Ethel bad only because she'd never had anyone to show her how to be good? Well, maybe so, I thought, surprised.

Ethel tugged at my arm and then she took hold of my hand. This time I let her do it.

8

"Girls, I'd like to talk to you both about what we can do until Monday," Momma announced at breakfast Friday morning.

I let my spoon hang in midair while a chill rippled down my spine. What now?

"We've all made an effort, I believe, to be courteous and proper whenever we go out." Momma glanced at Ethel. "The four of us, I mean. I have to admit, however, that there are some people around who don't exactly understand why Ethel is with us."

I wanted to say "amen" to that, but Momma sounded so serious that I kept my mouth shut. "Sooo," she said slowly, "do you think it would be a good idea if we didn't go to the movies tomorrow night?"

Alberta spoke up first. "You mean you're tired of people bothering us about Ethel, right?" Two red dots came out on Momma's face, but she only nodded. "Well, fine with me," said Alberta.

I felt so relieved. "Good! But what about church? We gotta go to church?"

"Only if you want to," Momma told me.

"But what if we want to be with our friends?" Alberta said. "And what about our softball games?"

"Oh, I'm not saying that we have to stay in the house with the curtains pulled." Momma smiled a little. "It's just—"

"You don't want to get in another fight," Alberta broke in.

"Let's just say that unless we all want to go someplace, you girls can go without me and Ethel. Just let me know first."

That sounded great. All this time I'd wanted to go over to Gloria's, and was afraid I'd have to take Ethel. Course, there were hardly any other girls my age who lived in town, and the ones who did, like Angeline, were ones I wasn't ever going to speak to again. Not after the way they teased me in church.

I liked Lizzie Carlton, but she didn't even have a telephone, so it was hard to get to her. She wasn't as good a friend as Gloria, but she worked when Gloria wasn't speaking to me, you know?

"Well," said Alberta, getting up from the table, "I think I'll call Evelyn and see if she wants to do some shopping."

I thought hard. "Oh, I guess I'll call Gloria and maybe we can go bike riding."

Alberta came back a few minutes later. Evelyn wasn't at home, Sandy had cramps, and Georgia was out of town. When I called Gloria, her mother said she was downtown with Sarah and Missy Walker. So after all that, Alberta and I ended up on the floor of our room, trying to teach Ethel how to play Monopoly.

Ethel landed on St. James Place and should have paid me fourteen dollars rent, but since she couldn't count, do you know what she did? Tried to give me a one-dollar bill! "Put your piece back on the board, Ethel, and pay me," I told her.

"No." She poked out her lips.

"You gotta play the game right," said Alberta, who was sitting on a big pile of money.

"No!" Ethel hit the board and knocked pieces everywhere.

I started to push her, then remembered that maybe she didn't know any better. "Just give me this ten dollar bill and four of these, please," I said patiently.

"No! Gimme the dice! I wanna play Nopoly."

"How come you talk like that? It's Mo-nop-po-lee," I tried to explain.

"*You* used to say Nopoly, Margie," Alberta laughed.

"And when you hit Daddy's property you didn't want to pay him, either."

My cheeks burned. "You're a liar."

"You're a double liar and if you call me a liar again, I'm telling. I quit!" said Alberta.

So we put up the Monopoly game. Ethel wouldn't help. She was starting to get rowdy and evil, kicking her legs back and forth on the floor, making squeaking sounds with her sandals. "I bet you miss your momma, don't you?" Alberta said to her.

Looking down at the floor, Ethel nodded and began to cry. That was when I really started to feel sorry for her. I'd probably go crazy if Momma just left and I didn't have Alberta or Daddy around, and didn't know where they were. It was easier for me to feel sorry for Ethel if I thought about myself being dumped some-place.

"You wanna play in my sawdust pile?" I asked.

Ethel nodded again, and a little smile came on her face.

We went down the path. My pile was out back, not far from the old coal shed. The sawdust from Daddy cutting firewood for Miz Moten and other folks had been there as long as I could remember.

I flopped down at the edge of the sawdust heap and pulled out my cooking gear, which I kept handy. "You know how to make pies? Just put what you want in this"—I handed her a TV dinner tray—"and mix it up good with water. You can make a meringue, too, with blossoms."

Ethel went for that! She ran back and forth to the house to get water, found a stick and poked around in the sawdust until she hit real dirt. She mixed that in with the sawdust. I made a pie, too, but it didn't take me long. Mostly I sat back and watched her. Ethel pulled a handful of dandelion blossoms and stuck them on top of her pie. "That's pretty good," I said.

"I'm gonna show Momma."

"Hey, wait a minute." As she started to get up, I grabbed her by the shorts. "You can't call my momma 'Momma,' cause she's not yours."

"Can, too!"

"No, you can't!" I almost hollered, but I made myself stop in time. "Call her Miz Carson, you hear?"

"Okay," said Ethel. She shifted her pie from one hand to another while she glanced back toward the house. "Can I show her now?"

I guess Momma liked the pie. Ethel was grinning when she finally came back. I used to show Momma what I made but I was too old for that stuff now, unless it was really good.

"Maybe tomorrow we'll go look for some fishing worms," I told her.

"Oh, goodie!" Ethel cried. Hunting worms wasn't any big thing, but I guess she was excited.

The first thing I heard the next morning was Ethel's voice. "Wake up, we gotta get some worms!"

I rolled over and looked at the clock. It was after eight already. I remembered that I had promised her we would go. We got out of bed and Ethel managed to struggle into her T-shirt. She pulled her shorts on backward, though.

"You gotta take those shorts off. You got 'em on wrong." She stood there staring until I pulled her shorts down around her ankles. "You gotta step out first."

So we got her clothes on right and I threw a brush over her hair and we finally got outside. "It's kinda late to look for worms, so we're gonna look for crickets," I said.

"How we gonna catch crickets?"

Now I don't really know one thing about crickets. Daddy could catch them, but I don't remember exactly how he did it. I think he'd put bread crumbs in a jar by the lumber pile the night before and the next morning there'd be millions of crickets inside that jar. "We just catch 'em with a jar," I said, trying to look like I knew what I was talking about.

"Crickets are nasty," Ethel said, making a face.

"Oh, come on, girl. Crickets are good bait."

"Good as grasshoppers?"

"How'd you know about grasshoppers?"

"Daddy said so," she replied.

I thought she meant my daddy, and that made me

mad. "You don't know Daddy, so he couldn't tell you nothing! Just stop lying, girl."

"No," Ethel insisted, "*my* daddy."

My mouth fell open. I didn't know about this business. "Who's your daddy?"

Ethel got down on her knees and thrashed around in the weeds. "There's a grasshopper!"

"I don't want any grasshoppers today. Who's your daddy?"

"You can tie strings around their necks and hang 'em. That's fun."

I sniffed. "Only little kids do that."

"Well, Daddy showed me how," Ethel said, with her nose in the air.

I tried again. "What's his name?"

"Daddy," Ethel said.

"No! His real name!"

"Daddy."

I sighed. "You're stupid, girl." Well, it proved she had a daddy. But I thought everybody knew their daddy's name.

When we got back in the house, I saw Momma fixing pancakes. And I was hungry! She had made the big ones that could take you an hour to eat.

"I bet you can't eat even one whole pancake," I said to Ethel as I poured sugar syrup over mine.

"Can, too!" Ethel grabbed a pancake in her hands, and syrup ran up her arm.

"Honestly!" said Alberta.

Momma went over and cut up Ethel's pancake. "I should have done this for you earlier, honey," she apologized. "Now you can use your fork."

I tried not to laugh. I hadn't seen anybody eat a pancake with their fingers except babies, and they didn't know any better. But I guess maybe Ethel didn't, either.

Alberta said slyly, "You used to do that."

"And so did you," Momma told Alberta.

I grinned at Momma, glad that she had taken up for me. Daddy would have.

I kept thinking about Daddy all through the weekend and how he would have done this or that compared to how Momma did it. I guess I really missed him.

We all got along all right, even Ethel, but when Monday morning arrived, I had one thing on my mind: Miz Mary was supposed to come back today.

After breakfast Alberta and I began to clean up the kitchen. Momma put on her gloves and picked up her trowel. She was on her way outside to weed her flower bed when Alberta stopped her.

"You haven't heard from Miz Mary, have you?" Alberta said.

"No, but I presume she's coming tonight," Momma said.

"I betcha she won't," Alberta said.

"And why don't you think so?" Momma stared at her.

"Because," Alberta replied, "the last time I washed dishes at Miz Orange's, Miz Orange said Miz Mary wouldn't ever come back."

"Miz Orange need not poke her nose into our affairs." Momma paused and then muttered as she went out the door, "Oh, ye of little faith!"

Alberta scowled. "Momma would believe anything Miz Mary says."

"Miz Mary said she'd be back, too, so there." I had to defend Momma. "Miz Orange is just talking."

Alberta added, "Girl, I could tell you some things about Miz Mary."

"Like what? That she's really, truly not coming back?"

Alberta hung the dish towel on its hook. "No," she said. "I mean— Well, forget it."

Just then the telephone rang and Alberta sprang to get it. "Momma," she hollered out the door, "it's for you. Long distance collect." Alberta covered the receiver with her hand. "Speak of the devil. It's Miz Mary."

A few minutes later Momma came into the kitchen with a bad-news-again look on her face. "The kitchen looks nice," she began, running her fingers over the stove. Then she said, "Ethel, your mother just called."

Ethel hopped up. "I wanna talk to her, too."

"Oh, honey, she was in such a hurry," Momma said sadly, "but she said to tell you that she loves you and misses you and will be home soon."

"How soon?" I asked. I got the feeling that it wouldn't be today.

"I'm coming to that," Momma told me with a little

irritation. "She said she couldn't get back tonight, but she'll be here for sure Thursday."

"Oh, Momma!" Thursday!

Ethel sat down hard on the floor and slowly shook her head. "My momma been gone a long time," she said.

Of course Momma had to go and hug her. I just stood there. I guess I felt a little left out because Momma didn't hug me or say it would be all right. I looked up to the doorway at Alberta when she cleared her throat.

"Your momma's too busy in St. Louis, Ethel," Alberta said.

Momma glared at her. "Alberta, please."

I couldn't understand something. "What's Miz Mary doing in St. Louis? Getting money for Miz Silk's store? Seems like she could have got it by now. Did she have to get a job?"

"She can only work at one thing." Alberta giggled.

"One more word out of you, Alberta," Momma warned. She ignored me. "Ethel, don't you like being here with us?"

Ethel nodded, but she still looked sad. I put up the broom and slouched out the back door so I could sit under the peach tree and think, but Ethel followed.

"Let's make sawdust pies, c'mon, Margie!" she begged.

I sighed. "Okay."

9

Thursday finally rolled around, but by noontime there was still no sign of Miz Mary. She must be having problems, I decided. She was supposed to come back two Sundays ago, and then this past Monday. Well, I had lived through all those days. And she was supposed to come back *again* before today ended. If I had a buckeye, I could rub it for good luck and make sure Miz Mary would get herself back home.

I was sitting out under my peach tree when suddenly

I had a frightening thought. Daddy might come back any time now. What an explosion there'd be if he came home and found Ethel here! As much as I wanted to see him, I didn't want him and Momma to get into another fight over Ethel.

I wondered what my life would be like with a real younger sister. Course, she wouldn't be anything like Ethel. A regular younger sister would be all Black and not trashy. Her parents would be Momma and Daddy, not Miz Mary and somebody. Who in the world *was* Ethel's father, anyway? The way everybody went around whispering, they had to know! It finally hit me that maybe everybody knew who he was but me! I had a right to know, too. After all, his kid was in my bed.

Alberta thumped down the path. When she got close, I said, "Do you know who Ethel's father is?" She looked at me funny and halfway shook her head. Then she got to staring down at the grass and pulling on her hair. "What's the matter with you?"

"Nothing," she said.

"So why are you acting so funny?"

"Just thinking about what it'd be like to live with Billy Ray."

"You ain't old enough to get married. You can't even date, especially not Billy Ray. You're lucky Momma lets you talk to him on the telephone."

Alberta sighed, loud as the paint factory whistle. "I didn't say *marry* him. I said live with him."

"Well, Billy Ray doesn't want you. He wants to play

Ping-Pong and ride his bike." Alberta couldn't cook, anyway, so how could she get married? Once she tried to make hamburgers and they came out red and squishy on the inside and harder than tree bark on the outside. "Can Billy Ray cook?"

"Can he cook? Who cares?"

"Somebody'd have to. You can't. He better cook or you'll starve to death."

"We could go to restaurants."

"They don't give out free food."

Alberta narrowed her eyes at me. "Those things are so minor."

"He gonna sleep in your bed with his towel and his funky feet?"

"Oh, Margie!" Alberta stood up. "I'm going to Sandy's." As she walked away she added, "And don't ask to come along. You gotta play with Ethel. We don't need two babies around."

"Who's a baby?" I went flying up to the house. If Alberta could visit somebody, I could, too.

When I came in, Momma was mopping the kitchen and Ethel was at the table eating lunch. Momma didn't like mopping. She said she didn't have to scrub floors when she was a child, and because of that had never learned right. Looked like she was beating the kitchen floor to death, banging stuff around and slopping suds everywhere.

I waited a few minutes until she looked up. "Can I go over to Gloria Hinkle's?" I asked.

"Go ahead, honey," she grunted.

"Can I go, too?" Ethel asked.

"No, not this time," Momma told her.

I went into the living room, where Alberta was whispering on the telephone. Her legs were crossed and she had wrapped half her hair around her fingers. "I get to go to Gloria's," I said, patting her on the shoulder. She jerked away from my hand, but I just giggled and went out and got on my bike.

When I got to Gloria's, Miz Hinkle said she wasn't home. "She and Sarah went to town. How's things at your house, Margie?"

"Fine." Miz Hinkle has dark circles under her eyes all the time. I used to believe it was makeup.

"How's your momma?"

"Fine."

"And Ethel still there? How she doin'?"

"Fine."

"Yeah, and she's gonna be there, too," Miz Hinkle said. "Tell your momma to call me so I can talk some sense into her head. Now you tell her I said that, too."

Boy, I hated to have to listen to stuff like that. Grownups sure liked to try to get gossip about Ethel out of me. I wished I could tell Lizzie Carlton what was happening. I wished I could tell Gloria, too. But with Lizzie too far away and Gloria not able to keep a word to herself, I had to hold in everything.

I rode over to the old house around the corner from us where I had first learned to ride my bike. The building was three stories tall and the second story had a balcony, but it was so rickety-looking that nobody dared to walk under it.

I walked my bike up the narrow driveway. Weeds grew up and down in the middle, but they weren't that high and I wasn't scared that I'd see snakes. I thought that Mr. Benjamin might come around today to cut the grass for Mr. Craft, who owned the property. I hadn't talked to Mr. Benjamin in a long time. I listened but I couldn't hear his tractor.

"Hey, Margie, c'mon here and talk to an ole man." There was Mr. Benjamin!

He was sitting at the side of the house on some cement blocks under an oak tree. I pushed my bike over to him and plopped in the grass beside him. He always wore the same clothes—blue bib overalls with the bib and straps hanging down, an ole torn T-shirt with a huge smear of dirt where he always wiped his face, and an ole black felt hat. He kept his hat pushed way back on his head.

"Hey, little miss, how you doin' today?" He stretched out his leg, reached into his pocket, and pulled out a little mayonnaise jar. "Too hot to cut that grass right now." He took a big swallow from the jar and wiped his mouth with the back of his hand. "You been good?"

I nodded. I knew some kind of whiskey was in that jar. "I just thought I'd drop by here."

"Yeah, yeah. This kinda weather's good talkin' weather. Now I know you don't want none of this mayonnaise. Did I ever tell you about John and that bear?"

Mr. Benjamin knew a million stories. Sometimes he forgot he told the same ones to me before, but I didn't mind. I loved to hear him talk. So I shook my head.

"Now ole John was just a dumb ole colored man. Well, he *acted* like he was. Well, one day Massa said, 'John, we got to build me a log cabin with a door so strong nothin' can get in and nothin' can get out.'"

Mr. Benjamin got to his feet, threw his head forward on his chest, and rolled up his eyes. "Ole John said, 'Yessuh, I'll build you a cabin.' Well, they worked and they worked." He swung an imaginary ax against the oak tree. "Chopped and chopped and rolled logs till they got that cabin built.

"Massa said, 'John, you got to get us a bear so I can have a bear rug.'"

Knowing what came next, I wrapped my arms around my knees and nodded.

"John goes up in the mountains, just walking, throwing them legs up high in the air. He walked and he walked till he finally got on the trail of a bear. So he followed that trail until he came upon the bear sleepin' right smack in the middle of the path! John lifted up one of his big feet and wham! Tromped that foot down on the bear's paw! Ole bear reared up with a roar, arms out all the way to here! Claws and teeth gleaming like swords!"

I could just see that ole bear's teeth ready to bite John to pieces. "Go on, Mr. Benjamin, go on!" I shouted.

"John flew down that mountain, bear hot after him! John hollered, 'Massa, oh, get the bear off me! Open that door!' John was flyin' and hollerin' with this bear behind him snappin' and roarin'. Ole Massa didn't want to open the door. Ole Massa was scared."

"And what happened then?" I asked. This was the best part.

"Just as John flew through the yard with that bear two inches off his hind parts, ole Massa opened the door!" Fists doubled up, legs pumping in the air, Mr. Benjamin had John running at the door. "But at the last minute, ole John veered to the left while the bear went right on in the cabin. John sprang around, closed that cabin door he built so strong nothin' that came in could get out. Locked ole Massa and the bear inside!

"Ole John said, 'Now you hold him, Massa, and skin him and I'll go get you another bear!'"

I rolled and laughed like I did every time Mr. Benjamin told that story. Mr. Benjamin made me see ole John doing all of those things.

"'And skin him and I'll go get you another bear!'" He always had to repeat the last line and laugh and shake his head. "Well, little missie, I done got some talkin' done. Now I guess I better do the same with this grass cuttin'."

"Thanks, Mr. Benjamin. You gonna cut all the grass today?" I didn't want him to leave.

He said he was. He climbed back onto his mower.

"You stay back good," he said as he pulled away into the weeds.

I was almost glad Gloria hadn't been home. Missing Mr. Benjamin would have made me sad. Alberta didn't like him, but I did. He and Miz Moten were the only grown-ups who didn't ask me a bunch of crazy questions. I hopped on my bike and flew down the driveway. The wind was pulling at my braids. I held tight to the handlebars so the tires wouldn't slide and flip me off into the gravel like that first time. I pretended I was ole John with that bear right behind me, snappin' and growlin' and rearin'.

When I got back home, Alberta was still sitting by the telephone. But she wasn't talking. "I thought you were going to Sandy's," I said, falling down on the couch and fanning myself with a magazine.

"And I thought you were going over to Gloria's." She made a face at me and then slapped her bare feet up on the wall. "Oh, shoot." She poked out her lower lip and sighed hard. "This ole place is *so* dead! No drive-in. No skating rink. No bowling alley. The ole folks got their ole taverns and clubs, but we can't do anything but go to church and play softball. And yes, I know, we got softball practice this afternoon."

"Momma wouldn't let you go to a drive-in."

"You don't know that. I wish we could move to St. Louis or Atlanta. Have something to do there."

I didn't care about any drive-in. I was hungry. I went

back to the kitchen, where Momma and Ethel sat at the table. Momma held a crayon and Ethel did, too. Mine! I wanted to ask how come that girl had my crayons, but I didn't. It wouldn't do any good to ask. I just made myself believe that Momma wouldn't let her break them up.

"Momma, Gloria's momma wants you to call her. She said she wanted to talk some sense into you."

"I beg your pardon?"

"She—she said she wanted to talk some—some sense into you," I stuttered. "I guess about Ethel."

Momma frowned. "What you don't know about, you might not want to try guessing at."

There was just no way to get around Momma. I made myself a sandwich and hurried into the living room to watch cartoons. But before I could even get to the television, Alberta flounced up and switched on one of those old draggy movies.

"I wanna see cartoons!"

"Well, I don't." Alberta lay down on the couch and pretended she'd been watching the movie for hours.

"Momma! Momma? Momma, Alberta won't let me see—"

"Margie, would you please stop screaming at me!" Momma hollered back. "Alberta, let her see what she wants."

Well, you know I was pleased about that! After the cartoons came *Martie Magician.* Alberta threw her magazine to the floor. "You don't watch anything that can teach you intelligence." She yawned and stood up, sliding her hands down her ole skinny hips.

Alberta had nerve, as dumb as she was in history. I couldn't see why she had to get smart at me. So I was surprised when she turned right around and offered to buy me an ice pop on the way to softball practice.

Boy, I raced out of that house, got my bike, and had pedaled out of the yard before I realized that it was kind of early to go to softball practice. But I didn't worry about it.

For sixty cents the Dairy Queen sold a foot-long ice pop. "Hurry up!" I shouted to Alberta, who was almost a half block behind me. Lots of times we raced, but this time she rode slower than one of those circus bears.

"You go inside. I'll pay from out here," she said when she finally got there.

I shrugged my shoulders, went in, and got my ice pop. I sat down at a table so I could concentrate on eating. Alberta sat down outside on a bench. Although I had three napkins, strawberry-flavored juice still ran down my arms and onto the table. I fought with sweat bees and gnats buzzing around. They all wanted my pop.

While I was eating, guess who rode up? Billy Ray! His ten-speed sure was an ugly bike. He had draped lavender fur strips between the spokes of the tires and over the handlebars. A long bike flagpole swayed in the back, but instead of a real flag, a St. Louis Cardinals baseball pennant hung from it. Strapped to the bike bar was a little radio and tape recorder. That radio was playing loud, too.

It hit me suddenly what Alberta was up to. I bet she had planned to meet him here! I could see her outside sitting with her legs crossed. As she talked to that ole stupid boy, she took fancy little nibbles off her foot-long. I knew she was blinking her eyes real slow at him, too.

When Billy Ray finally rode off, Alberta stood up and looked after him like he was on his way to war. As soon as I came out she snapped her head around and asked, "Are you ready to go to practice?"

"Momma's gonna—"

"I said, are you ready to go to practice?"

So we got back on our bikes and went to practice. After we came to the field, I had another thought. "We didn't tell Momma where we were going."

"Momma knows when we practice." She laid her elbows on the handlebars and rested her head on her hands.

"She didn't know we were going to the Dairy Queen first."

"She'll be able to figure that out from looking at your sticky arms." She glared up at me. Boy, did she ever look evil! "And, Margie, there's no law that says people can't stop at the Dairy Queen. So before you go blabbing to Momma about Billy Ray, remember that a

Dairy Queen is a public place and anybody can go."

"I don't care about people going to Dairy Queens. But I bet you told Billy Ray to come, and I don't want to get in trouble."

"If you open your big mouth to Momma," she said angrily, "you're gonna end up with a knot on your head!"

I worried about that for a while, but since there wasn't anything I could do about the Dairy Queen business, I just stopped.

Practice was terrible. Coach was late and that made her mad, so she yelled at us when she got there. When Georgia and Evelyn dragged in even later, Coach made them run fast five times around the bases. They giggled and stumbled around, which made Coach madder. Sandy couldn't pitch the ball with the right arch, and then she got the giggles, too. Flies and grounders thumped and rolled around the field, and everybody just gawked and laughed.

Gloria and I sat in the dugout and watched our team fall to pieces. "Must be a full moon," Gloria said.

"Full moon?"

"Momma says when the moon gets full, people go crazy, especially on the weekends. They start shooting and drinking and fighting. This is only Thursday, and just look at them fools."

"I hope they don't act like that tomorrow at the game," I said.

"Momma went crazy this morning." Gloria laughed. "My sister Livvie was banging the vacuum cleaner against everything and Momma said, 'Be careful.' Livvie rolled her eyes and started mumbling about how nobody could do anything right around her."

Gloria flicked her hand out toward my face. *"Whap!* Momma smacked Livvie and said she was tired of her sass and she'd be glad when Livvie was grown, 'cause she was tired of trying to raise an ole hot-tailed girl."

"What's hot-tailed?"

Gloria looked crafty. "You know what 'the hots' is, don't you?" she asked. I nodded, though I wasn't sure. "Is ole Stinky Pete still at your house?" she asked suddenly.

"She ain't stinky!" My cheeks started to burn.

"Well, I see you know who I mean, so she still must be there," Gloria said.

Much as I disliked having to listen to Gloria tease me, you can believe that I wasn't in a hurry to get home. I was sure Miz Orange or somebody had shuffled along and seen Alberta with Billy Ray at the Dairy Queen. And they'd probably seen me. If they told Momma, she would have a fit! I could just see her standing on the front porch with a switch in her hand and a lecture in her eyes. Alberta knew Momma didn't want her sneaking around to see Billy Ray. Why did she have to drag me into this?

But practice ended and Alberta and I got on our bikes. Alberta went cruising off home like she didn't

have a care in the world. I didn't have any other place I
dared to go, so I followed.

I soon saw Momma and Ethel on the front porch. I
didn't see a switch, but Momma didn't need one; she
could beat you to pieces with her words. I slowed my
bike down until I was pushing myself with my feet.
Goose bumps popped out on my juicy arms.

Alberta leaned her bicycle against the house. "Hello."

"Hello, Alberta," said Momma.

Alberta went up the steps past Momma, but I hopped
onto the porch from the side, out of her reach. The
porch sure was hot! Don't ask me any questions,
Momma, I prayed, because I sure don't want to answer
them.

Just as Alberta touched the screen-door handle,
Momma spoke up. "Just a minute. Where've you been,
Alberta?"

"Softball practice."

"I must not have heard you say good-bye."

Alberta put her hand on her waist. "You know we
always practice on Thursdays if we don't have a game.
And before we went to practice we went to the Dairy
Queen. Margie wanted to go, too. We bought foot-
longs. We rode our bikes. We went—"

"That's enough!" Momma sounded like she was boil-
ing. She stood up. "When you get eighteen you can
come and go as you please. I told you before that I don't
mind your going places. But you still have five years to
give me the courtesy of letting me know when and

where. And I warn you, don't be sneaking around with no-account punks!"

I watched their eyes lock. Then Alberta went into the house, slamming the door. With Momma in that mood, I knew I was going to get it. I wished I could crawl under the house. Momma must know about Billy Ray! Or did she?

Ethel patted Momma on the arm. "You mad?" she whispered.

"Somewhat," Momma said, glancing over at me.

"My momma can get mad," said Ethel. "She can cuss and holler and jump around. She says I'm a pain in the butt—"

"Ethel!"

"—and she's gonna drop me down in a well and let me drown. Then she won't have no more trouble." Ethel was talking like she was just reciting her ABC's. "Momma says then she could go out and dance with Daddy whenever she wants to and not have to sit around with me."

"Oh, honey," Momma exclaimed, "your mother doesn't mean that."

Ethel put her big gray eyes on Momma and went quiet again. I was so surprised about Miz Mary wanting to drop Ethel in a well that I forgot about my own problems. Momma sat down and talked with Ethel about Miz Mary and everything. Then she looked at me.

"Margie?"

My leg jerked. "Yes, ma'am?"

"Did your coach make you practice hard?"

"Oh, Momma!" I was so relieved that the words leaped out of my mouth. I told her about Coach being mad and the team acting stupid, everything!

"My goodness," said Momma.

"Does the full moon make people crazy?" I asked. Momma raised her eyebrows. "What?"

"I thought maybe that's why Alberta was acting so funny. Gloria said the full moon made people do crazy stuff and she said her momma said that Livvie was hot-tailed and I thought maybe that was what was wrong with Alberta."

"What?" Momma asked, frowning.

"The moon hasn't done anything to me," I added real quick. I didn't want her to find out about Alberta and Billy Ray being at the Dairy Queen together. "I don't like to chase boys." But I knew I still said something wrong, because Momma jumped up and shot into the house.

I turned to Ethel, scared I was really gonna get it either from Momma or Alberta. "You wanna play jacks?" I asked.

I tried to send Ethel into the house to get the jacks, but she wouldn't go. I peeked in the kitchen. At first everything was quiet. Then I heard Momma say, "And get off that telephone right this minute! You don't know who you're playing with, sister!"

I hurried into our room, got my jacks, and came back

outside to play with Ethel. After we got tired of that, we made sawdust pies until Momma yelled at us to get ready for supper. I didn't go sit in the kitchen like I sometimes do, because Momma still sounded mad. Ethel and I went into our bedroom to find something to do.

"You still got my seashell?" I asked her, not figuring that she did.

"Yeah." Ethel dug under her pillow and brought out the shell. "And I got Alberta's, too. They got their own beds."

During dinner Momma and Alberta didn't even look at each other. Their forks clinked loud on their plates. I don't like no-talk dinners, so I said to Momma, "Ethel learned how to play jacks, kind of. And we made more pies."

"I'm glad to see you and Ethel hit it off." Momma sounded like she was just answering me, and hadn't really heard what I said.

The telephone rang. Alberta jumped away from the table like it was on fire and left me sitting there with my mouth hanging open. "It's for Momma," she called out in a few minutes.

Momma was on the telephone for about ten seconds. When she returned she lit into Alberta again. "I told you that you can't go out with him and that's what I mean. I forbid you to even talk to that boy. If I hear about you being seen with him again, I'll make you stay inside this house for a whole month!"

Alberta's eyes and cheeks were red and her voice

sounded fuzzy like bubbling Seven-Up. "May I be excused?"

"Certainly."

When my eyes got big, Momma said, "Since I don't want you to start performing, too, I'll explain what your sister's so mad about. I heard about Alberta being at the Dairy Queen with that boy Billy Ray. Sneaking around! Then she had the nerve to tell me she wanted Billy Ray to take her to the movies."

"Just her and him?"

Momma nodded. "He just now called to ask me directly because, as he put it, 'The man of the house ain't home.' The nerve! And he got the same answer Alberta receives each time she asks—NO! She knows she can't date until your father and I say so."

"Alberta always told me only Daddy could say when she could date, and he said she couldn't until she was fifteen."

"That's true," Momma said. "But don't forget that I have quite a lot to say about it, too. That's why she keeps pestering me. She thinks she can wear me down, I guess."

Boy-crazy thing, I thought scornfully. Alberta slobbered over that Billy Ray the way she used to over softball. Until a couple of months ago she had been in serious training for softball. No pop, lots of sleep the night before the game, sucking on sugar cubes for energy between innings. But she had hardly even oiled her glove since Daddy left. And I saw her eat only one sugar cube at our last game. I guessed that now she was in training for boys.

I didn't want to think too much about Alberta and Billy Ray, though. I reminded Momma that Miz Mary was supposed to come home tonight.

"That's right," Momma said with a warning glance at me. When she saw I wasn't about to make a face, she smiled a little. "Ethel just might be going home tonight. Her mom won't recognize her little girl."

I peered at Ethel. "She is a little browner."

"Oh, but she's changed more than that, don't you think? She doesn't spit beans on the floor. She's become a very well-behaved four-year-old."

Just then Ethel caught on to our conversation. "I don't wanna go home," she said.

"You'll have to when your momma comes," I said.

"No!" Ethel shrieked. She kicked the table.

"There, there, Ethel," Momma said gently. "Let's just drink our milk, okay? Drink your—"

"Don't wanna—"

"I need for you to drink your milk," Momma said quietly.

Ethel glared at me, but I looked away. I didn't want to get into this fight any more than I wanted to get into Alberta's. Out of the corner of my eye I saw Ethel drink her milk.

"How come you don't want to go home?" I asked when she had finished.

"'Cause." Ethel looked at Momma and then at me.

" 'Cause you-all got pretty things. 'Cause Momma here ain't said she was gonna throw me in a well. And she ain't beat—"

"Oh, Ethel!" Momma got up and went over to Ethel. When Ethel began to cry, Momma wrapped her arms around her. "Oh, honey, that won't happen. Poor baby."

I couldn't imagine any mother wanting to throw her kid in a well. No wonder Ethel thought our house was heaven.

Alberta refused to leave her room, even when Momma called for her to help me with the dishes. So I washed the dishes and dried them and put them away.

Later Ethel and I sat on the front porch steps and played jacks until dark. "Where does that come from?" Ethel asked, pointing at the moon brushing the treetops.

"It just pops up from somewhere," I said.

We sat there in silence. After a while Ethel said through her fingers, "I like you."

I watched the moon slowly rise up. "You better go on to bed, Ethel." And just like that Ethel headed for the door. "And you're okay, too, when you act right," I added.

"I been good," Ethel said. "Ain't I?"

"Yeah, I guess so."

I thought I could sit outside all night, but I was too tired. I staggered into our room and groped around in the dark for my pajamas.

Just before I went to sleep I heard a faint muffled whistle from a freight train. It moaned like it had lost something. It floated over that patch of trees around the old Black cemetery out on Turkey Creek road. It echoed over the highway, the countryside, all over Missouri. Trying to find somebody. Maybe that whistle and maybe the full moon would bring Daddy home. And Miz Mary.

10

When I woke up the next morning, I wasn't surprised at finding Ethel there. I guess she was starting to just be part of my bed. For now, of course.

"I'm gonna show you how to really catch worms," I said. Since it was Friday, I wanted to make sure we had plenty of worms in case Daddy came home.

We walked through the wet grass and Ethel pointed to a cardinal perched on the coal-shed roof. "Birdie's singin' howdy-do," she chattered.

Well, right then, her loud talking should have tipped me off. Ethel got to stomping around scaring everything. "Don't walk so hard," I warned her. "The worms'll hear you." I stabbed my shovel in the ground by the blackberry bushes. Between two pads of moss two earthworms were pressed together, mating. I was so embarrassed! I guessed they were hot-tailed, too. It was poor taste, Momma always said, to bother mating things, but I still couldn't resist. As I reached my hand down, they pulled apart and slipped into their holes.

"When we gonna go fish?" Ethel asked.

"Maybe tomorrow," I whispered. "Don't talk so loud. Besides, you probably won't be here to go with us."

Ethel frowned up. "I don't wanna go home. No, I wanna stay here with you and 'Berta and Momma— Momma Carson."

My mouth fell open. That was the first time she'd ever called Momma something other than Momma. She was really learning! So I said real nice, "It'll be too bad, but you gotta go when your momma comes."

"No! No! No!"

"Okay, okay! Shhh! Look, I gotta find some worms, else we can't go. Let's look some more."

So Ethel squatted down and peered around the bottom of the bushes while I dug in the weeds. I hit worms about half a shovel down.

"Margie!" Ethel squealed. "I found you a worm!"

Ethel wasn't too terrible at helping me, though I had to show her how to do everything. In fact, she was almost as good as Alberta on a worm hunt. Now Momma would say that Ethel and I had something in common. I guess we did. Worms! Maybe when Miz Mary came back I could go get Ethel to help me once in a while, if I felt like having her around.

When we got into the house, Momma glanced in the can. "You got such big ones I'm not sure I want to touch them. Bugsie Malone!"

We giggled. Momma always called worms Bugsie Malone after a worm she saw in a cartoon. After snapping a plastic lid on the can, she slipped it into a bag and then set it in the refrigerator.

"I don't have anything against worms," she explained to Ethel, "but I don't want them sliding around in my lettuce or eating the meat loaf."

Momma hummed a boogie tune as she set a basket of clothes on the floor and turned on the washing machine. "What're you going to do today, Margie?" Momma asked.

"I thought I'd go to the library."

"Would you take Ethel with you just this once?" she asked. "I need to get these clothes done." She wrinkled her nose at my dirty underwear.

"I don't know." I tried not to frown up.

"Ethel, have you ever been to a library?" Momma wanted to know.

Ethel shrugged. "What's a 'brary?"

"Li-brar-ree," I corrected her, after a glance at Momma. "It's where you borrow all kinds of books to read. You gotta bring them back, though, and you gotta take good care of 'em."

"Don't want no books."

"Well, you can't read, anyway." I saw Momma frown, so I added, "But you can look at the pictures. They got pictures of all kinds of animals."

Ethel eyed me like she didn't believe a word of it. "Wanna see a 'lephant."

"Elephant?" Momma laughed. "So go see elephant pictures. You'll love the library, honey."

Momma told Ethel to be proper and courteous at the library while I stood there listening and chewing my lip. I'd never taken Ethel anywhere without Momma. Why did I have to start now? What if she mangled a bunch of books or got in a fight or ran away? What if she jumped in front of a car or got bit by the Sherwoods' dog, Rex? Or threw a rock through somebody's window?

"Momma, can't you come, too?" I pleaded. "Ethel might not pay attention to me like she does you. Please?"

"But almost all our clothes are dirty." Momma flapped her hands at the washing machine. She looked at me and back at the clothes. I made my face look real sad. "Well, okay." She started to unbraid her hair. "But you better not say anything if you run out of clean panties. Would you ask your sister if she wishes to honor us with her presence?"

Relieved to know that Momma would come, too, I hopped and skipped into our room, then very carefully woke up Alberta. When I asked her if she wanted to come, she sat up and said real low, "I guess so." Both sides of her face were wrinkled from sleep and her eyes looked fat from crying.

While we got ready, Momma fixed breakfast. I ate so fast she had to look at me twice. But I was in a hurry. This early in the morning only a few folks would be out downtown. So maybe there wouldn't be anybody for Momma to stop and talk to. See, I didn't want her to get in another fight.

The grass in Miz Moten's yard glittered with dew, even though the sun was up. Two big maple trees grew in the front, so everything was shady. Then we had to walk across a field with a little grass path for a sidewalk. Mr. Patai and Mr. Cranshaw owned the property, and on both sides of the path they grew rows and rows of sweet corn. It was about up to my waist. I wished they would build a sidewalk.

Hunched between the Phillips 66 gas station and the big concrete drainage ditch was Miz Orange's square, gray house, which reminded me of a prison. When we came up to it, I saw that Miz Orange was sitting on her gray front porch in her rocking chair. Her hair was rolled up in rubber curlers under her hairnet. A radio and a television were on in front of her. She talked on the telephone with the receiver snuggled between her head and shoulder. Extension cords were going every-where. All that just to keep up with the gossip.

Alberta, who hadn't said a word to anybody since we left, suddenly turned to me and whispered, "I bet she's got some more nasty dishes waiting on me. Well, I'm not doing them today."

We came up to the porch. Well, Momma did. "Good morning, Octavia," Momma said.

Eyeing Ethel, Miz Orange hollered at Momma, "Mary ain't come back yet, has she? It's Luvenia Carson," she said into the phone. She turned back to Momma. "Going downtown, are you? Yeah, she's going downtown," she said into the phone. "Sure, she's still got that gal! Oh, hush your mouth, Maudie!"

Miz Orange hung up and sat back. "And how you doin', Margie and Alberta?"

"Fine," we mumbled, and shuffled a little distance away. Momma went up onto the porch and began to talk up a storm.

"Oh, shoot," whispered Alberta, "let's go ahead. Momma just talked to that ole woman yesterday. All they do is talk. And this dust is getting in my hair."

"What dust?" I didn't see any tractors around, and it wasn't windy.

We heard Miz Orange say, "Bet that woman's still over there chasin' after him."

"What woman chasing who?" I whispered to Alberta. But Alberta just made a face and kept quiet.

Momma and Miz Orange kept talking. Just when I figured we'd have to wait all day, Momma and Ethel came up. "If you could drive," Alberta said to Momma, "we wouldn't have to stand around in this heat waiting so long."

"Well, I wouldn't drive any twenty miles just to take you to some dance in Lancaster," Momma replied, "and you can believe that."

Well, they were still fighting. I hoped they wouldn't get into it in the middle of the sidewalk with Miz Orange right there on the porch. I wished Alberta would stop doing what she was doing to make Momma mad.

We passed the Swensens' laundry. A clock that hadn't worked for years hung from a post outside. Ethel stepped under the clock and stared through the window at Miz Swensen. Miz Swensen just stared back. Smiling a little at the woman, Momma gently pushed Ethel away.

"Don't like her," said Ethel. As she flopped along by Momma, she kept looking back toward the laundry.

"If you don't watch where you're going, you're going to stub your toe," Momma told her.

"I ain't gonna stub no toe," Ethel snapped.

In three more blocks we would have been safe, but suddenly I saw Missy, Sarah, and Johnny on the other side of the street. Alberta saw them, too. She reached into her macrame purse, took out her sunglasses, and arched them on her nose.

"This town is just too small for privacy," she complained.

I tried not to look across the street. I was sure they would see us and start to get smart. But they just went into the drugstore. "Whew," I said to myself. I might be getting used to Ethel, but it still wasn't easy for me to have people my and Alberta's ages see me with her. I didn't want them to think that Ethel was ours forever.

Finally I saw the faded, red bricks of the library. As soon as we were inside, Ethel marched right to the front desk. "Wanna see a 'lephant," she said.

"Shh," I told her. "You gotta be quiet in here."

Miz Agnes, the librarian, scooted back her chair and stood up. "Now, Margie, you keep good watch over that child," she warned, "and don't let her tear up here like she did with Miz Silk's beautiful patterns."

"Yes, ma'am."

"You don't have to worry," said Momma slowly and clearly, with just a note of hatefulness. "Ethel is with us. There'll be no problem. And we will presume," she stretched out that word, "that you won't find any."

"Well, I know you have fine girls." Miz Agnes sat back down. "Sure is heating up quick outside, isn't it?"

Ethel scampered around until she found the picture books, which were kept in a little cubbyhole kind of room near the back. She held her hands together tightly, I guess to keep from touching anything. Well, at least she's trying, I thought.

When I was little, this was my favorite room. On one wall were painted muscular, sharp-faced men in blue work pants swinging sledgehammers at railroad spikes. Strong, iron-colored thunderclouds hung behind them in a lavender sky. The paintings were called murals.

"Look at these pictures, Ethel." I felt very teacherly. "All this stuff was drawn by ole-time artists." The

murals reminded me of the movies we saw during vaca-
tion Bible school, with lots of Black people working on
the railroad.

I sat down on a tiny chair by Ethel and opened the
first elephant book. "What the 'lephant doin' in that picture?" She traced her forefinger over the elephant's
trunk.

"Taking a bath. 'With a nose like a hose, he can clean
his toes,'" I read. "And he can keep cool with the
water."

Ethel gritted her teeth and squeezed her eyes shut.
"Cool ole 'lephant, water comin' out his nose." She
peered at the next page. "What ole 'lephant doin' there?"

"'Eating leaves from the trees in the African
breeze.'" I read on and Ethel listened. She became so
quiet I could hear her breathe and swallow.

In came Alberta. She fell back against the wall and
watched us, looking evil.

"'Berta look like a 'lephant," Ethel said laughing.

Like an ole turtle Alberta snapped, "Shut up,
Ethel."

"Girl, we're not bothering you," I said back. I could
almost smell her frying over there. When Ethel tugged
at my hand, I turned another page and continued to
read. Under Alberta's sizzling glare, we finished the first
elephant book and picked up another. I'd never seen
a kid get so happy over an ole elephant.

Then Momma poked in her head. "We're going in a
few minutes," she said.

"Want another 'lephant."

"I'm gonna check out some elephant books," I told Ethel. When she stayed frowned up, I added, "That means we can take some home for a while."

"Want some 'lephant now!" she whined. "I don't wanna go!"

"Ethel!" Momma was sharp. Ethel closed her mouth.

"Momma, I gotta find some books for myself, too, okay?" I hurried away, glad to be out of the room, and nearly ran into Momma's favorite person. Standing in the biography section was Billy Ray Morgan. I skidded on my heels and whirled off in the opposite direction. I wondered if Alberta knew Billy Ray was here. I sure hoped Momma didn't.

When I came to the front desk, Momma was talking with Miz Agnes. Alberta slouched by the door. Ethel, her head propped back, stared up at Alberta. "What 'lephant eat?" she asked her.

"You!"

"Alberta, that's enough!" Momma warned.

"Oh my," said Miz Agnes.

"I beg your pardon?" snapped Momma.

Quickly Miz Agnes turned to me. "Margie, you're gonna be a tired-eyed girl, reading all those books," she said. "You sure love to read, don't you?" She took her little red pen and scribbled in the date for me to get the books back by, and then let me write my name on the cards.

Outside, the morning was already sopping with humidity, and by the time we got home, so was I. Momma stomped up the steps and knifed her key into the lock. The screen door cracked like a gunshot at her back.

"What's Momma mad about now, Alberta?" I asked.

"I don't know and I don't care."

I bet, though, that it had something to do with Billy Ray being at the library.

"Alberta, I want to see you now!" Momma's voice, ice thin, chilled my eardrums. I hoped that she wouldn't make Alberta stay home from the next softball game. But boy, was I glad she didn't holler at me like that!

I didn't find out what had happened between Momma and Alberta until that evening at the game. The game was in the second inning and we were up to bat. Alberta and Sandy were huddled together in the dugout, whispering and smacking on gum.

"She said I couldn't go," I heard Alberta tell Sandy. "I told her it wasn't even a date, with you and everybody else being in the car." She stopped whispering and got loud. "But she said she didn't trust Billy Ray's brother driving."

"Umph, umph, umph, you just can't do nothin', girl."

"She's so old-fashioned," Alberta went on. "And she talked like Lancaster was a million miles away. It's just an ole dance, anyway. You'd think I was trying to go to some whorehouse."

She turned and saw me looking at her. "I guess we'll

be on TV, Sandy, there's the broadcaster." She and Sandy laughed, then they strolled over to the water fountain.

Alberta had no right to call me names. I wasn't a gossip! She wanted everybody to hear, anyway. She was just trying to be smart, smacking on that gum, twisting her ole skinny behind around everywhere, talking about Momma.

I just decided to watch the game and try not to pay any attention to Alberta. Picking up the bats had been no problem. Coach had bought a new bat and everybody used it. Maybe that bat was doing the trick for us. We already had fourteen runs and it was only the third inning. The other team, Second Baptist from Winefield, only had six.

I watched Alberta trip around drinking a can of pop. I knew she hadn't picked up any sugar cubes from home, either. She must have just quit her training altogether. That girl was off her rocker.

Our team went back on the field. Near our dugout, boys with braids on their heads roamed around rubbing their stomachs under their shirts. Just then I saw Billy Ray ride up on his dumb bicycle and start talking to a girl on the Second Baptist team.

I didn't care if she talked to that fool Billy Ray all night. But when I glanced at Alberta on first base, I could tell she was so mad, she was ready to bounce all over the field.

"Well, I heard some ole yellow heifer had a thing for you," the girl said. I saw her nod over at Alberta. Boy, did I get mad! Calling my sister names! "Some ole high-yellow heifer that's got some ole half-white kid staying with her," the girl said loud enough for everyone to hear.

"Who you calling a heifer?" Alberta jumped off first base, threw down her glove, and walked stiff legged over to the girl.

"Alberta!" Mr. Oscar, the coach's husband, hollered at her, but Alberta went right on.

The girl looked Alberta up and down and laid her hand on her hip. "If the shoe fits, wear it. I don't see nobody jumpin' around like un ole dried-up yellow thing but you."

Well, right in the middle of the game Alberta and that girl got to arguing and cussing. Everybody poured off the field and from both dugouts to see. I nearly got trampled trying to get over to Alberta. The coaches were shouting, people were coming down out of the bleachers, and boys were running from the sides of the fields. It looked like those old riots I saw on TV. Momma was standing up with her mouth open.

"Don't start no stuff that you can't clean up!" Alberta yelled. She had her fists balled up and her whole face was red.

"Well, if you think you can kick my butt, then, honey, come on!"

Alberta pounced on that girl and they both went down, rolling in the dirt. Fists and arms and legs were going every which way. I pushed and tried to get through to help Alberta, but everybody was pressing in too close. And then I heard a heavy, booming voice that made everybody stop:

"Now just what the devil is goin' on?"

It was Daddy! Daddy was back!

11

He had got here just in time. I saw him jerk folks away left and right. He reached down and grabbed that girl from on top of Alberta and snatched her to her feet, and then he grabbed Alberta and shook her straight. It got so quiet, I almost keeled over just watching him.

He stood there in his bib overalls and his red-black-and-green knit cap holding those stupid girls. "I said, what the devil is goin' on?"

Alberta's hair, full of dirt and sand, was sticking up all over her head. She plucked at her torn T-shirt halfway up her chest. I could see the bottom of her brassiere. The other girl was in just as bad shape as Alberta.

Still nobody said anything. My heart beat so rough my shirt must have been poking out every other second. I didn't care. I forgot all about the fight. "Daddy!" I kicked and pushed through those people and wrapped my arms around him as high as I could reach.

"Well, brother, you sure know when to come back," somebody said to Daddy. Then people got to laughing and talking to him and making jokes about the fight.

The Second Baptist girl tried to twist herself from Daddy's grip. He let go and watched her walk off a few feet before he said, "Next time you-all wanna fight, go to the dog pound, you hear? Hunh?"

The girl mumbled something as she walked away. Alberta just nodded. Momma got down to us then. "Alberta!" Her palms were up in the air like she was trying to catch rain. "What in the world?"

"Just let it alone for now, Luvenia," said Daddy. "I think we better go home."

People started to walk away, talking and laughing. Daddy let loose of Alberta and swung me up in the air. "Hey, Bitty Bit! How's my lady?"

At last we were a family again! Daddy was home!

Like honeybees, questions buzzed inside my head. What should I tell Daddy first? Exactly when would he make Ethel leave?

Smiling at Daddy, Momma said, "Let me get Ethel so we can go."

Daddy didn't say a word.

"Daddy, I'm gonna give you a thousand hugs," I said.

He smiled and hugged me, but he was watching Momma. "And I got a million for you, lady."

Our run-down red Chevy sat behind the bleachers. I still loved it, too. Just when I got ready to grab that seat behind Daddy, Alberta pushed past me and flung open the back door. She sat down in *my* seat, dropped her glove beside her, and smiled at me wickedly.

"Alberta," I started to shout, "you better stop pushing! Gimme my seat!" But she didn't move.

Ethel climbed in on the other side and stuck her arm out the window. "You gotta sit in the middle," I told her.

"Don't wanna," she answered and stayed put.

Momma slid onto the front seat. Daddy lit his cigar and puffed until smoke clouded around his head. "Margie," he said, "you sit by the door so she don't fall out."

Ethel pouted, but she scooted over and sat on Alberta's glove until Alberta snatched it from under her.

Our Chevy took off with the same familiar thump in the motor. "You-all sure know how to give a welcome-home party," said Daddy. "I'm afraid to ask if my girls have been good."

"I have!" I said. I knew Alberta had no right to say a word, after that fight. "Momma says she's proud of me. She says I got maturity and understanding."

"Me, too!" Ethel squealed.

I frowned. What was Ethel doing, acting like she was one of Daddy's girls?

"Alberta and Margie have been pretty good," Momma said slowly. "Of course, there's a few little kinks we have to get straightened out."

Daddy cleared his throat. "No lie about that."

Daddy certainly would straighten out those kinks, I told myself. He'd make Ethel go home, and take care of Alberta's craziness over wanting to date. "Ethel broke up my seashells," I told him, "and she peed—wet—in my bed twice and spit—"

"Busy girl," Daddy murmured. I saw him turn his head to look at Momma. For a few seconds nobody said anything. Finally Daddy said, "I figured you girls would be having a game. I just got back from Arkansas. Soon's I took that truck back to Gillespie, I shot my ole Chevy straight home. Nobody there! Well, then I remembered that you-all might be out at the softball field."

"Oh, I hope you didn't speed, Matt," said Momma.

"Daddy knows how to drive," Alberta said real smart.

"Say what?" Momma turned around in her seat.

"She say Daddy can drive," said Ethel. "Ow!"

"Alberta's pinching," I said. Then I heard a hiss: "Shut up, Miz Broadcaster."

"Alberta sure has something on her mind," said Daddy. He drove the car into our front yard. The grass had grown over his parking place. Momma usually said that driving on the grass was country, but this time she was quiet.

As Alberta opened the car door, Daddy said, "Hold on just a minute. Now what exactly have you got on your mind, Miz Professional Boxer? Miz Muhammad Ali?"

"I got plenty on my mind." Alberta flounced out of the car, went into the house, and slammed the screen door behind her.

Daddy sighed. Cigar smoke drifted around both ends of his mustache. "You got something on your mind, too, Bitty Bit?" he asked softly.

"Yeah. Ethel." Tears came to my eyes. When he talked soft to me like that, I could tell that he understood the terrible things that had happened to me while he'd been gone. "Daddy, she's—"

"Let's go inside, Bitty Bit, and let this ole man stretch out his legs," said Daddy.

When we got in the house, Momma asked, "Are you hungry?"

Daddy sat down on the couch. "Is a pig pork?" He laughed, but stopped abruptly when Ethel parked herself on the floor smack in front of him and stared up at him with her mouth open. I didn't care for her to sit so close to him, but I didn't say anything.

I crawled on the couch beside my father. He wore those same old work shoes, but when he had left they had looked halfway new. Now the leather was stained, and the laces were knotted. Daddy had been driving hard.

Just then Ethel jumped up and claimed the couch on the other side of him. He stopped talking to look at her. I frowned.

Ethel didn't need to crowd up on top of him! She really began to get on my nerves. She wasn't family. She was just a guest, and a stayed-too-long guest at that. Daddy was home now. We were running on family time.

"Miz Mary's been gone for ages," I told Daddy. "She said she was gonna—"

"I bet Daddy's got so much to tell us," Momma interrupted. "Tell the girls where you've been."

"You know I just got back from Arkansas. I went to Tennessee. Drivers gettin' sick all over." He was eating some chocolate pie and chocolate ice cream Momma had brought to him. "I didn't go to California. Family got scared and said they didn't want to have their house fall down from an earthquake. I even went over to St. Louis to see Uncle Jake."

"Oh, Uncle Jake!" I shouted. "Is he gonna come see us?"

"You never know about Uncle Jake," Daddy said. He looked at Momma, and Momma looked down at the floor. Daddy handed me his bowl for more ice cream.

When I got to the kitchen I looked around to see this little frizz head behind me. Ethel! "Gettin' ice cream for Daddy," she said, grinning.

"He ain't your daddy; he's mine." I was so tired of her! "And *I'm* getting him ice cream, not you." Ethel frowned at me, then stamped out of the kitchen. Good, I thought. Only one person was needed, and that was me. But if Ethel thought she could take my place, then, honey, try it!

Back to the living room I marched. Alberta had done it again! She had her ole skinny behind where I was sitting.

"I'm sitting there, Alberta." I handed Daddy the bowl. "Better get up. Daddy, make her move."

But Daddy patted Alberta on the knee and said, "Take turns. I'm not going anywhere."

"But she took my seat!" I stamped my foot and jiggled my legs. Enough was enough. "Well, Ethel, you gotta move."

"Bitty Bit, come sit by me on the floor," said Daddy.

So I sat down on the floor, hard, to show my disgust, but nobody even noticed. When I leaned against his knee, Momma told me to sit up.

"What part of Tennessee did you go to?" asked Momma.

"Memphis. That's one big ole country town, falling all over into the Mississippi. But it's pretty." Daddy put a stern look on his face. "Miz Alberta, what's the capital of Arkansas?"

I pulled on my braid. I knew it was Little Rock because I'd learned capitals this year. I could tell Alberta didn't know because she was dumb in geography.

Alberta found a bored look to replace her evil one. "I don't know."

"You might go to the bathroom and see if it's showing," he told Alberta.

"See if what's showing?"

"Your behind. Margie, what's the capital?"

"Little Rock!" I said proudly.

"Little Rock!" shouted Ethel.

I leaned over and made a face at her.

Daddy ate and ate and talked and talked about his travels, and Ethel followed every word he said. I snorted. I bet she didn't have any idea what he was talking about. He wasn't talking to her, anyway. Ethel made me sick.

After a while she fell asleep against his arm. I must have shown my disgust, because Daddy stopped talking to ask, "What are you tearing up your face for, Bitty Bit?"

Alberta snickered. "Because Ethel's snoring all over you."

"Ethel's got a crush on your Daddy," Momma told me.

"I guess I've been wiggling my lips so much I must have wiggled her to sleep," Daddy said. He looked at the clock. "Hey! It's after midnight. I'm tired. Time to go to bed."

I bounced on the floor in dismay. I hadn't even had a chance to talk with him, with that Ethel always in the way. But maybe he'd have to go to the car and get presents; that way we could talk if he let me go with him. I thought real fast. "What'd you bring us?"

He just winked. "That's a secret. Now you sweet things get on to bed. Give me kisses. And, Momma, get that baby to bed."

Alberta, right there on the couch beside him, got the first kiss. But when it was my turn, I hugged and hugged on him until he had to laugh and push me off.

I slipped on my pajamas and dumped myself into bed. Momma kissed us all and turned off the lights. In the dark, I lay there and tried to figure out why I felt so funny inside. There were usually good surprises and good feelings and lots of jokes and laughing when Daddy came home. But this time seemed different to me. Ethel being there must have made things seem so strange.

And Ethel! All evening she had been the perfect kid, smiling and cuddling up to Daddy. I thought I'd been perfect, too, but he'd hardly said a word to me. I thought about that for a while, and then it hit me: Ethel knew her momma didn't want her, and now she was trying to sneak into our family. That went through my head real hard two or three times, and boy, it really made me mad!

But there was something else even worse: Ethel already had Momma. And now she was after Daddy. If she took Daddy, then I wouldn't have anybody at all.

All of a sudden I didn't care about Ethel adjusting or

being well behaved. I didn't care if Miz Mary beat her or threw her in a well. She wasn't gonna get hold of my daddy. Not for anything!

I rolled over and glared at that trashy kid sleeping in my bed. "You're not gonna get my daddy. Better go find your own!" I raised my fist and brought it down hard on her back. "Never!"

Ethel whimpered once, but she stopped real quick and just lay there. "Never," I promised myself.

12

"Sister Alberta," said Daddy at breakfast, "how old are you now? Sixteen going on twenty-one."

"You know I'm only thirteen. Wish I was twenty-one." Alberta wrapped strands of unbraided hair around her forefinger.

"Bet you do, too, but you ain't. Aren't. You and Momma have been gnawing at each other something terrible, so I hear. And last night you had the fists going.

I want to hear what you got to say, get this out in the open."

Alberta hesitated like she was trying to make sure she had her story straight. "Billy Ray wants to take me to a movie and Momma said no," she began. "And a bunch of kids are going to a dance in Lancaster and I asked to go, but she said no again. And I don't think it's fair, 'cause it's just an ole movie and an ole dance. Momma can't drive us to the dance 'cause she can't drive, but she won't let me go 'cause Billy Ray's brother is driving. Sandy and everybody are going to the dance but me."

"But I don't care what Sandy and everybody else do, Alberta." Daddy set down his coffee cup. "I'm talking about you. And I don't see where you got to be going crazy over some dude like Billy Ray." Alberta frowned and sighed so loud that Daddy had to put his eyes on her real hard. "You blow like that again"—he got to laughing—"and you'll take everything off the table. I didn't have to go to California to get shook up by an earthquake. I got Hurricane Alberta."

Before I could stop myself I got to laughing, too, and a piece of scrambled egg flew out of my mouth. Daddy was always saying funny things. He never got upset like Momma did.

Daddy cleared his throat. "How about I run you and Billy to the show?"

Alberta was so surprised! Then she grinned real sneaky at Momma, who didn't change the expression on her face. She just kept on eating and smiling a little.

"And," Daddy added, "we'll all three see the show together."

"What?" Alberta screamed.

"He can sit on one side of you and I can sit on the other." Daddy smiled at Momma and his mouth twitched. "You're thirteen. You were thirteen yesterday and you'll be thirteen tomorrow. You'll be fourteen next year and after that fifteen, and then if Billy Ray wants to party with you, fine. By then I hope he's got that towel off his shoulder and some sense in his head." He leaned toward her across the table. "You can think I'm old-fashioned, but you ain't goin' with him alone. Frown up all you want."

Alberta threw down her fork. The clatter of the metal against her plate rattled everybody.

But Daddy spoke in the same tone of voice he'd been using all along. "You break it, you'll pay for it," he said. "You've been carrying your behind up on your shoulders a little too much. Don't let it drag too low, though, because I'm right behind you in size twelve boots."

He and Alberta eyeballed each other until Alberta had to look down at her plate. She fiddled with her fork and finally picked it up. "I can't be going out with anybody and my father right there," she said in a real small voice. I could tell she had to fight to keep her crying from gushing up.

"Then maybe your idea of a date and mine aren't the same. Want to tell me your side first?" Alberta shook her head. "You wanna go to that dance? I'm going with you. You ain't gonna run wild like a jackrabbit in the desert 'cause someone else does. I ain't no fool. I grew up in the country with nothin' to do, too."

"Then I don't wanna go."

"You know for darn sure I ain't taking Billy Ray by myself," he said.

Good enough, I told myself. This was something! Momma always tried to shut us up when we argued with her or acted like she didn't hear. I guess she got that from Grandmother Ralston. Not Daddy. Well! And now I was hotter than ever to know what he was gonna do about Ethel.

Daddy pushed back his chair. "I got an—"

The doorbell rang and Momma went to answer it. "Maybe that's Miz Mary," I said to Daddy. It was hard for me to see the door, and I couldn't hear a thing.

"You're gonna get your neckbones out of joint, Bitty Bit," said Daddy, "stretching and peeping like that."

Momma came back and gave a piece of paper to Daddy. He looked at it and sighed, glancing at Ethel. Then he said, "My announcement!" and knocked his knuckles on the table. Ethel squealed and hit the table, too.

"Aw, cut it out, girl," I said angrily.

"Number one," said Daddy, "I have a new job. As of Monday I'll be district manager of the moving company in Gillespie. And that means . . ."

"C'mon, Daddy, what?" I asked, eager to know.

"That means I can drive to work and be back home every day!"

Home all the time? Whoop for joy! I sprang out of my chair to hug Momma and Daddy. Daddy home for every breakfast and every dinner and every weekend! Home just to be home, falling out asleep in his chair or on the couch, fishing every weekend, going to church and the softball games and taking me everywhere he went!

"Wait now." He got to grinning. "And first thing Tuesday we're getting another car."

Even Alberta came out of her sulk to ask questions. "A new car! Like maybe an El Dorado?" she said.

"And, Momma, you can learn how to drive," I added.

"Maybe Momma will and maybe Momma won't," she said, grinning. "I still like to walk. But maybe with this new car you won't have to be a mechanic to get it to start."

There was no more mad shouting or fighting. I was even able to forget a little about Ethel still being here. So what if Ethel laughed with us? She didn't matter anymore because she would have to go soon, probably tonight if not before. I felt a little bad that she might have to go to the Children's Home until Miz Mary got back. Well no, I didn't feel too bad. I could always go visit her, you know.

Daddy put on a mournful look. "Don't I get kisses?"

I hurried to plant the first kiss. Alberta just sat there.

Daddy raised his eyebrows at her until she finally slouched over and hugged him. Ethel climbed out of her chair and held out her arms to my father. "Me, too," she said.

Daddy told her, "I guess I can get a kiss from you, too."

I stamped the kitchen floor hard with my foot. "He's just saying that 'cause you're a guest," I snapped.

"Margie, shame on you," Momma said.

Daddy looked at me, but he only said, "And now I got to go fishing. It's not too late to catch a few. Those worms you got, Margie, must be ten feet long."

Ethel butted in. "I got worms, too!"

"But I got almost all of them, Daddy." I made a real evil face at Ethel. She wasn't going to start that lying around Daddy.

Sandwiches and fruit had to be packed. Poles had to be readied. Clothes had to be changed. I raced around the kitchen but Alberta took her time. "Fishing is country," she said.

"I can't find my sandals!" Ethel hollered from our room.

"Margie, go get her sandals," Alberta ordered.

"You go get 'em."

"I gotta make sandwiches."

"Well, I do, too."

"You better or I'll tell Daddy you and Miz Hamlin got into it."

"Well, I'll tell about you and Billy Ray at the Dairy Queen."

"I don't care. Doesn't make a bit of difference to me what you tell."

I glared at her, and then I ran to the bedroom. Next Ethel wanted a glass of water, but she couldn't reach the glasses on the kitchen shelves. "Margie, get her that glass," said Alberta.

"How come I gotta do everything?"

And then Ethel wanted her own fishing pole.

Phooey on Ethel! Having to run errands for that ole kid made me mad. "You don't need a pole 'cause you don't know how to fish!"

"Do, too!"

"Well, I'm not gonna bait your hook and Daddy won't have time!"

"Ease up, Bitty Bit." Daddy came out of their bedroom in front of Momma. "Everybody ready?"

At that Ethel flew out the front door. I knew dead sure what was on her mind. "Firsties on that backseat," I shouted after her, but she jumped in the car and sat in my spot. "That's my seat! You better move!" I swooped around the back of the car and reached in.

"Gonna sit behind Daddy!" Ethel squealed, kicking at me.

I pulled at her. "He's not your daddy and that's not your seat! Go on home, white trash, half trash, tired of you hanging around us!"

A huge, brown hand closed gently around my arm. "Margie, you know better than to call names," said Daddy.

"Make her move! Alberta got it last night and I couldn't even sit by you on the couch." Tears sprang down my cheeks. "Make her go on home. Don't let her go with us!"

"It's all right for her to come fishing," he said. "Be nice for me. Say, get the worms, hunh?"

I could have killed Ethel. I stamped back to the house; I was that mad. But I also had this flat feeling inside me. Ethel was getting her way around Daddy like she had around Momma. Everything was going wrong, not at all like I thought it would be if Daddy came home and found Ethel here. I grabbed the worms and kicked open the screen door.

Before it could bang shut Momma caught it. "Ethel's never been around Daddy," she said in her ole teacher voice, "so she can't help but like him, too."

So what if Ethel liked Daddy? Everybody liked Daddy, but not everybody was trying to move into his house. I hated Ethel and her ole evil ways. When I got back to the car I saw that Alberta had put her behind in the seat by the other window. Nothing was left for me but the boring middle. All the way to the river I got madder and madder and worried more and more. Would Ethel never go away?

The Mississippi was rolling in thick waves today, stirring up mud everywhere. From out the car window the banks looked like chocolate. When the river was like this fishing was slow. Other days when I wasn't catching fish I would work on making mud bowls and plates. If I was careful, I could make a whole set of dinner plates and then put out scraps of bread on them for the river mice to eat. Sometimes I looked for buckeyes in the leaves lying on the ground. When I found one that wasn't wormy or cracked, I'd keep it for good luck, like Miz Moten said I should. Once I found a buckeye and the next day at the school raffle I won a free ticket to the Malco.

But with Ethel around, I didn't feel like doing much of anything. I was used to playing by the river with only my family around. I didn't want some little kid up under me chattering and asking stupid questions. I didn't expect anything good to happen today. Bad luck trailed me like that bear after ole John.

Daddy drove up to his spot on the river. In deep water out there somewhere was a good catfish hole. Around the weeds growing in the shallows were big bluegill, and under the rocks splashed by the current were bass like the one I caught last time.

"Everybody out." Daddy unlocked the trunk and lifted out cane poles, his tackle box, and his and Momma's river rods and reels. Well, right away Ethel knocked over the can of worms. Worms rolled around on the ground in one big ball until Daddy picked it up.

Then Ethel nearly got poked in the eye running back and forth around the poles. After she took off her sandals, she stepped on a cocklebur and screamed fit to kill.

To keep from going crazy, I decided to just ignore her. What else could I do? I went ahead and got my own pole ready, unwinding the line and checking the hook. Then I got ready for the worm. I hated for the worms to knot themselves up into a slimy ball. Balled-up worms! One look at that and for four nights straight I'd have nightmares about worms in my bed. I had a bad-enough worm ball in my bed already.

Daddy squatted near me. "I'll get you a worm." I was thankful for that. "Want me to bait your hook?" he asked.

"I can do it." I was going to show him that I was no baby like that whining Ethel. But the worm fought back. It wrapped itself around my thumb, crawled over my fingers, and fell to the ground. I turned my back, picked it up, and pushed it onto my hook with a stick. "I'm ready!" I had to grin with relief.

Daddy and Momma baited up and flung their lines far into the river. Ethel pulled at Daddy's leg all the time. I was so disgusted. "Wanna fish, too," she whined.

"Go ahead. Get that pole there."

She fumbled with the pole, then threw it down and stuck out her lips. "Pick up the pole," said Daddy, but Ethel didn't move. "Pick up the pole." She did. "Now take the hook real careful. That sharp thing there is the hook. Don't jerk at it. Your fingers'll end up bait if you do."

Daddy just stood there and told her over and over what to do. He wouldn't go to her and help, and I was glad. "Undo the line," he told her. "Turn it, turn the pole to undo your line."

Ethel unwound the line like her hands were killing her. Daddy stuck a worm on her hook. "When the cork goes under the water, you got a fish," he said. "That red-and-white thing's the cork. Just jerk your pole all the way up, way up over your head." He tried to tell her how to throw in her line, but she got tangled up in it. "Momma, do something with this child before she throws herself in the water," he finally said.

When Alberta was handed a pole, she turned up her nose and said again that fishing was country. Then she switched away to a clump of bushes and sat down in front of them. Daddy frowned. I watched them. I hoped Alberta wouldn't make him angry.

Daddy put down his pole. "Alberta, let's take a walk."

Alberta still looked sullen, but she got up and followed him around the weeping willow trees.

With Momma's help Ethel finally got her line straightened out and into the water. But the worm was twisted up in the line, and the line was wound around the cork. "Lookie, I'm fishing, too, Margie," Ethel squealed.

"That's what you think." I saw Momma look at me, but I didn't care. Unless Daddy said something to stop Ethel, that kid was going to be hanging around me all day! My cork bobbed in the water. I had to leave off thinking about her to be ready, so I waited and it bobbed again. Snatching up the pole, I jerked it high over my head. The fish was gone and so was my worm, but at least I'd had a bite. Maybe I could catch a big one quick. That would show Ethel, all right.

When Alberta and Daddy returned, I was on my third worm. "Momma," said Alberta, "Daddy said I can go on to the show with Billy Ray."

"Did he, now?"

Alberta looked happier than she had all week. "Daddy's still gonna go, too, but at least he's not gonna sit with us."

"Well, I could have told you that," said Momma. "He was just joking, anyway."

"Why didn't you?"

"Because that was up to you to figure out. I would suggest that you just be glad that *we* are allowing you to go." Momma gave Alberta a long look, and then smiled at her.

I was glad Alberta got what she wanted, which was more than I had right now. I tried to concentrate on my fishing, but that was hard to do because Ethel was jerking up her pole and then she was throwing it in, and then she was jerking it out again. A million times a minute! It was easier for me to keep inching down the bank than to holler at her to stay away from me. But that was what I finally had to do, because she followed me down the bank, too. At least she didn't whine at me to bait her hook. She grabbed worms left and right and stuck them on her hook like she knew what she was doing.

When I got to my fifth worm, Alberta came over. She was acting regular again at last. "Getting any bites?"

"Yeah. You're not mad 'cause Daddy's going to the show with you and Billy Ray?"

"Sure I am, sort of. But it's better than sitting around at home. Besides, with Daddy back for good, maybe he'll let Billy Ray drop by the house. And see, I'll work on Daddy and I bet you I get to go out without Daddy with me before I turn fifteen." She primped at her hair.

I just stared at her. "And Daddy said for me to stop sliding on my chest because I might hurt my breasts," she went on. "He just wants me to prove to him that I got common sense, see."

"Did Daddy say anything about Ethel going home?" I asked. But Alberta didn't answer. She just put her head down and then she went right over to Ethel and helped her work with her pole. I didn't like what was happening at all. It was like knowing Rex was finally going to chase you, but you didn't know if he would bite you, too.

"Ole fish down there is stealing my worm," said Daddy. He put another worm on his line and cast it out. "Oh say, Margie, we gotta talk. I haven't had a good talk with you in a long time."

Finally! Me and Daddy together! He'd been saving me for last. Last meant most important. Now I'd get some satisfaction.

Ethel ran to Daddy. "Me, too!"

"We don't need you!" I shouted. "You can't go."

Ethel strapped her arms around his leg. "Gonna go, too!"

I threw down my pole as hard as I could. "You let go!" I doubled up my fists and headed for her. "Go on! Told you!" I smacked her hard on her arm. "Get away, get your hands off him!"

I hit her again and, dodging Daddy's hands, bopped her one smack in the nose. Pulled at her ole nasty hair. Daddy didn't know how evil she was, wetting in my bed, taking my clothes, even sitting in his chair while he'd been gone. I couldn't help it. I'd had enough!

Daddy pulled Ethel off his leg and got between us. "Make her *go!*" I kicked at Ethel. "We don't want her! Trashy thing! Tired of her! Make her go away!"

"Bitty Bit." Daddy tried to calm me down, but I kept on shouting. "Bitty Bit," he said, taking me by the shoulders, "I'm afraid you're gonna have to get used to her. Ethel's gonna be with us for a long, long time."

13

Without even thinking, I pulled away from Daddy and began to run. I ran as fast as I could and as far as I could away from Ethel, who had ruined my life, and away from Daddy, who could not understand. I ran down the ole path between the weeping willow branches, up past our ole red Chevy, and down into the bushes.

Everything was wrong! Everything was unfair! I should have figured it out and got myself ready for the worst. I should have known when Ethel first came flopping through our front door that things wouldn't ever be the same. I wanted to hide under these bushes forever.

Heavy steps thumped nearby and bushes rattled. I saw Daddy peering down at me through the leaves. "Can I come sit by you?" he asked. Without waiting for an answer, he lay on his stomach beside me. What did I care? I wouldn't even tell him that there was a tick in the grass right beside him.

"Everybody's been doing you wrong, haven't they?" said Daddy.

They sure were! But he could just go ahead and talk. Talk was all that he and Momma ever did. I guess he figured he'd better have his ole talk now because he'd be busy from now on with Ethel.

I didn't want to listen to what he said, but I did. "Momma's been so worked up over Ethel, and Alberta's gone nuts over some boy," Daddy said. "Then I finally come home, barely take time to say hello to you. And now I've let your worst enemy move into our house."

He could just keep talking. It didn't matter to me. I was that mad and upset and helpless. I watched the tick crawl on the ground closer to him, but I wasn't going to tell him.

"Ethel's all by herself right now, Margie. Miz Mary's skipped off and left her. Your Momma's been telling me how well you and Ethel've been getting along. Playing jacks, telling stories, fiddling with bees. You've treated her almost like a sister."

"She's not my sister!" I screamed. "Me and Alberta are sisters! But you say she's gonna stay with us and nobody cares how I feel!"

All of a sudden I got to crying, hard. I hurt from my head all the way down into my stomach. Everything bad that had happened swooped down on me and stung.

"Oh, yes, I do care," Daddy said. "I didn't mean sisters like you and Alberta are sisters. But like a relative. Did you know that Ethel is your cousin?"

"What? How?"

"Uncle Jake," said Daddy. He looked at me and smiled, but he looked sad. "Uncle Jake is her father."

"Our Uncle Jake?" Uncle Jake and Miz Mary? Everything turned upside down. It almost made me madder at the same time. I didn't want Ethel to be Uncle Jake's kid. I didn't want him to have anything to do with Miz Mary. I didn't want Ethel to be my cousin, and I *sure* didn't want her to keep staying with us.

"Ethel's just an ole, stupid, nasty, trashy thing! And everybody's been laughing at us and she broke up my stuff, but I got to share everything with her." I couldn't stop talking. "I've been waiting and waiting to tell you how terrible she's been!"

My eyes were hot and burning. Tears rolled hard down my face. "Ever since she came I waited for you to make her go. But she stayed and stayed, and now you're home but she's still gonna stay! Why does she get to stay with us? I don't care if she is my cousin!"

Daddy scooted closer to me, but he didn't touch me.

"I told you I went to St. Louis and saw Uncle Jake. Listen, just listen to me. I talked to him and I talked to Miz Mary. Now I didn't like the idea of your momma bringing Ethel home. And I didn't like her going down to Miz Mary's, because I don't approve of the way she lives in the first place. But the only reason your momma ever went there was because Uncle Jake asked her to keep an eye on Ethel."

"But when did Momma ever go down there?" I said. "Just that one time!"

"Sometimes she'd go after she got off from school. Not often. So when—"

"But—"

"Wait a minute, baby. So when Miz Mary decided to go tearing to St. Louis, it was because she was trying to see Uncle Jake, and Momma took Ethel in. Miz Mary was going to leave Ethel in the trailer."

When I kept on crying, Daddy put his arms around me. I tried to push him away, but he forced me up against his chest. He held me tight to him until I got tired of fighting and dropped my head against the strap of his overalls like I always do.

"Terrible to make these tears drop on the ground," he said real soft. "I bet you've been holding back tears ever since I left. Just cry your eyes on me, Bitty Bit. I'm back home."

So I cried. I cried about everything I could think of, but mostly I cried because I was going to have to share him with somebody else. He let me go on crying, too.

Finally I got tired of crying, but the feelings didn't go away.

"Miz Mary is one of those women who can't deal with taking care of what she's supposed to," Daddy said. He rubbed his beard across my forehead. It used to tickle. Well, it still did. I pushed my head up against his chin so he would do it again. "And Uncle Jake is like that, too," he added.

"I changed my mind about not letting Ethel stay after I thought about me not being around and *your* momma just running off and leaving *you*. When I put you in Ethel's place, I felt really bad. I would hate to let anything like that happen to you."

We just sat there awhile, the two of us. At least I had him to myself right now. There wasn't anything I could do about later on, though. It was gonna be Daddy and Momma and Alberta and me—and Ethel. When I thought about that, I wished I could cry some more, but I didn't have any tears left.

Daddy said, "People look at Ethel, who's half white, and they look at her momma, who's white and trashy. Miz Mary lays around guzzling booze. You know, sometimes Ethel wouldn't even get supper, and lots of times not breakfast. Her momma whipped her all the time. And often Ethel had to stay in that trailer by herself all night. Sometimes she couldn't get out because her momma would lock her inside. That's a sad thing, Margie."

He got quiet and I thought about what he had said. I

bet it was creepy being locked up in that nasty trailer. What if there was a fire and Ethel couldn't get out? I bet she could hear rats and hobos and everything scratching around outside, too. I didn't want to feel sorry for Ethel, but I guess I did. I wouldn't want to stay in that trailer by myself. Not even in the daytime.

I sure wished that Uncle Jake or Miz Mary had her. But they didn't. We did.

There was one more thing I had to tell Daddy, even though it was too late. "I waited and I waited." It was hard for me to breathe with my throat so sore from crying. "I waited for you every night and thought about where you were and wished you were home. And then you finally come home and I got to wait some more. Now I'm still gonna have to wait because Ethel's gonna hang around you all the time."

"What?" he said.

"Ethel just came in and took over all my stuff and now she took you, too!"

"Oh," he said slowly. "I see. No, that's not the way it is. I got plenty of love for you, baby. Ethel hasn't taken a thing."

"Yes, she has!" I was crying again. "Falling asleep against your arm and sitting right behind you in the—"

"No, Ethel hasn't taken a thing from you." He hugged me gently. "Not really. Families have been taking in kids for years." He sighed. "Lots of kids get strung out in the cold. Your mother is her aunt, you know. And I'm her uncle. She's blood kin."

"But it's not fair!" I had to make another try. "Uncle Jake and Miz Mary should have her."

"A whole lot of things aren't fair, Bitty Bit." He shook his beard over my face, but he didn't laugh or smile. "People should do lots of things, like raise their own kids. It's not any thrill for me to have another kid in the house. I'm used to just ole knothead Alberta and you. But some things won't change. People have to change."

He was talking about me. I tried to pull away, but he wouldn't let me go. He got to growling like that bear Mr. Benjamin talked about, trying to make me laugh. I didn't. But I felt a little better.

"You are mine, Miz Margie. You are your Daddy's lady and you're gonna stay his lady."

We sat there some more. The tick tried to crawl up his pant leg, but I flicked it off. Finally I said real low, "I bet you want me to deal with it."

"Well, listen to her," Daddy said. He hugged me, then turned me around so he could look at me. "Can you deal with it?" he asked.

I pressed my lips together. I knew what he wanted me to say. "Do I have to?"

He didn't say anything. He just smiled a little. Then I lay back against his shoulder. Maybe if I had trouble—and I knew I would—Daddy would help me out. Like now, with just the two of us. At least maybe I could talk to him when I felt bad. And I guess he could make things easier for me when Ethel got to be a pain.

A grasshopper jumped on a fern frond curling up near my feet. When I reached for it, it jumped away and instead my fingers dug into a thatch of matted leaves. I picked up the pile and dropped it on the ground. Two buckeyes rolled free. Good luck! Maybe a buckeye still meant something. I wondered if that ole stupid Ethel might want one.

Eleanora E. Tate,

like the family in *Just An Overnight Guest*, grew up near the Mississippi River in Canton, Missouri. She was graduated from Drake University, where she received her B.A. in journalism.

Ms. Tate has written for newspapers, magazines, and poetry journals. She has won a number of awards for her poetry, and has had her essays and short stories for children published in various collections, including *Off-Beat* and *Children of Longing*.

Ms. Tate currently lives in Myrtle Beach, South Carolina, with her husband and daughter. This is her first novel.